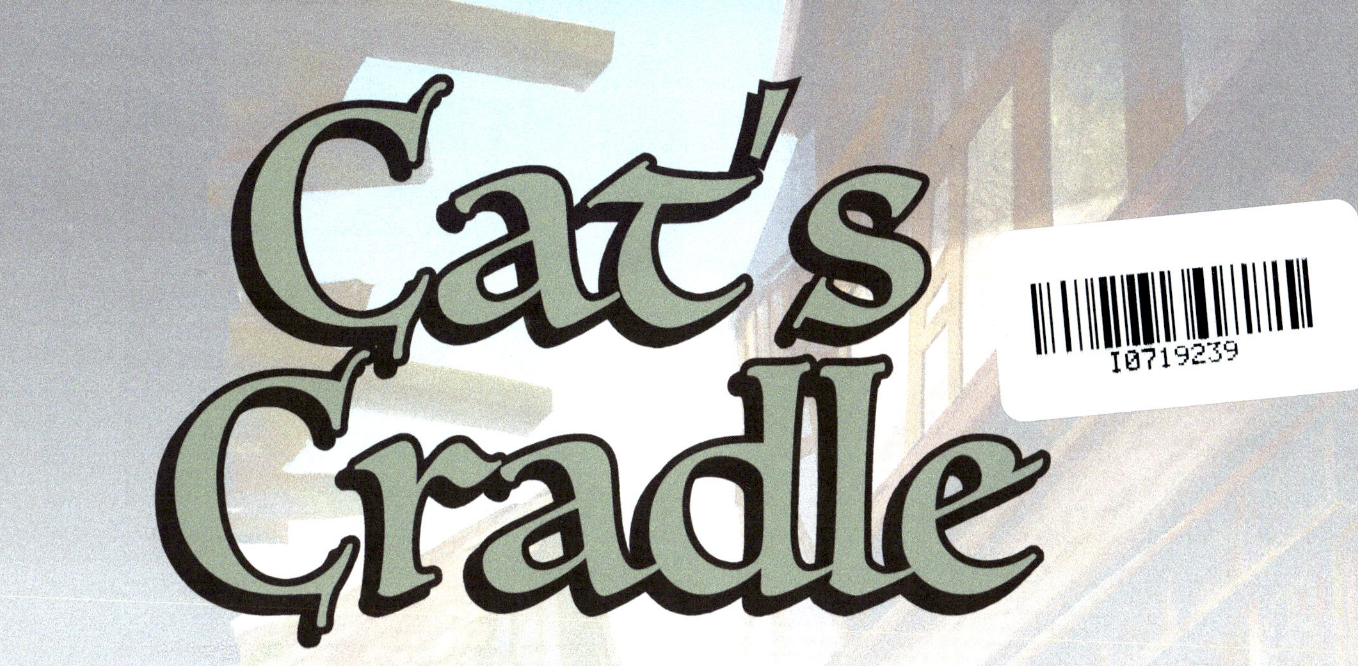

Cat's Cradle

Authors: Rhiannon Louve, Anthony Pryor, Matt Finch

Developer: Matt Finch

Editor: Jeff Harkness

Art Direction: Casey Christofferson

Layout and Graphic Design: Charles A. Wright

Cover Design: Suzy Moseby

Cover Art: Colin Chan

Interior Art: Bill Blakely, Colin Chan, Adrian Landeros, Thuan Pham, Sid Quade, Erica Wiley

Cartography: Alyssa Faden, Suzy Moseby

Fantasy Grounds Conversion: Michael G. Potter

Frog God Games is:

Bill Webb, Matthew J. Finch, Zach Glazar, Charles A. Wright, Edwin Nagy, Mike Badolato, John Barnhouse

FROG GOD GAMES
ISBN: 978-1-943067-85-5

TABLE OF CONTENTS

OVERVIEW

INTRODUCTION

Cat's Cradle is a small city with a population of approximately 5,100 — small enough that it is often referred to as a town. In the world of the Lost Lands, it is located in the Duchy of Saxe, at the intersection of the Gap Road and the Hyon River, but it can be placed anywhere that a caravan route intersects with a river trade-route.

The most salient features of Cat's Cradle are the mines of the Salchamp to the north (where various magically infused minerals used in alchemy are mined), the Quicksilver (a small stream that carries strange runoff from the Salchamp), and the town's main industry: alchemical supplies and products. Given the town's location on both river and land trade routes, these characteristics should supply you with a place that offers adventure hooks for as long as the adventurers choose to base their operations here.

It is also worthy of note that people in Cat's Cradle almost never seem to get sick from ordinary diseases, and that a large part of the city is in disrepair due to the use of "ripplestone" as a building material, a material that turned out to be alchemically unstable over time.

HISTORY OF THE TOWN

SEVEN CENTURIES AGO

Cat's Cradle began long ago as a simple keep — still standing and inhabited today — near the center of the city (though much-remodeled from its original form). Orshal, its founder and the first baron, and Volemar Assaro, his best friend, are local folk heroes, though little accurate history is known from their time. Over the next several centuries, Cat's Cradle grew ever larger, in part because the Quicksilver had carved out such a perfect docking area for traffic on the main river (the Hyon).

FIVE CENTURIES AGO

The little city prospered, eventually incorporating a small rival village on the other side of the Quicksilver. Remnants of this rival village can be found now incorporated into Cat's Cradle's Jade District. Sometime later, now centuries ago, a strange greenish runoff coming down the Quicksilver alarmed residents and led to the discovery of the ripplestone quarry and the Salchamp.

The Salchamp's discovery forever altered the course of Cat's Cradle's history, as the alchemical salts in these strange mines — more often referred to as the Salt Skeleton — transformed a small, sleepy town into a hub of alchemical advancement and trade. It is believed, though uncertain, that the inability of long-term Cat's Cradle residents to become ill stems from the discovery of the Salchamp as well.

ONE CENTURY AGO

The ripplestone discovery was less beneficial, as the decorative, marble-like stone eventually proved to not be particularly marble-like after all. In the time of Baron Scolren, the current baron's great-grandfather, it was discovered that the wealthiest area of Cat's Cradle, located between the keep and the docks, was crumbling dangerously due to extensive use of a poor building material.

Baron Scolren's tenure was marked primarily by the Ripplestone Exodus, during which most of Cat's Cradle's wealthy residents relocated across the Quicksilver to rebuild — with another newly discovered marble-like stone — to form the Jade District. Jade-marble, unlike ripplestone, was tested by alchemists before being put to use, so most believe that a repeat of the Ripplestone Exodus will not occur.

SEVENTY-FIVE YEARS AGO

While the Jade District was still being built, however, Cat's Cradle's docks were hit by a devastating alchemical fire, which caused another major

1 SQ = 500 FT
THE TOWN OF
Cat's Cradle
N
E
S
W
MAP S

blow to local trade. The Panhandle District was built after this crisis, and laws were passed to allow alchemical mixing only in the Baronial Corridor along the Quicksilver.

FIFTY OR SO YEARS AGO

Baroness Escaulla's tenure came next, and was mostly about rebuilding, as well as the growing of other industries in Cat's Cradle, including brickmaking and glass-blowing. Though her efforts to restore the city from the disasters of her father's time were largely successful, Escaulla died unpopular, both because of a perceived disconnection from the common folk of the region and because of the growing bandit army that attempted, in her old age, to wrest the Salt Skeleton from Cat's Cradle's control.

TWENTY YEARS AGO

Baroness Escaulla's son was Baron Escallel (Baron Scale's father). By the time he took stewardship of the city, Cat's Cradle's outer wall was complete, and its defenses were bolstered by forces from his liege. He ran a long but strategically excellent campaign against the bandits (the Salt War), destroying their leadership and scattering their forces. However, in an attempt to restore the people's faith in their baron, he insisted on leading from the front and actually battling the bandits in person. He died in battle with great honors, defending the Salchamp and succeeding handily in restoring his family's popularity. He was only 46.

YEAR BEFORE LAST

Baron Scale is a charming and ambitious young aristocrat, the son of Baron Escallel. He has been baron for only two years. He has a wife, Baroness Liera, and two small children. Though an excellent leader in his own right, Scale humbly credits most of his success to his wife and his still-living mother, Lady Resla.

Baron Scale's brief tenure has seen major economic and population growth for Cat's Cradle, almost entirely due to the baron's excellent administration. Scale is working toward the restoration of the crumbling, ripplestone-riddled (crime-infested) Old City and toward an ambitious bridge project — among other things — in the nearby village of Gambit.

LAW ENFORCEMENT

Crime and law enforcement are often the major theme of city-based adventures, that is when cities are not used just as the basic setting for buying unusual equipment or for making contact with patrons. Cat's Cradle has multiple law-enforcement agencies, which allows you to create adventures where the law might end up on both sides of a complicated situation.

Law enforcement locations include:
A-7. Baronial Disaster Brigade
B-14. Barretti's Rooms (a private investigator)
C-4. The City Courthouse
C-10. The Watch House
D-1. Baronial Constabulary
D-3. Cat's Cradle Port Authority
D-11. Eastview Tower
G-3. The Baronial Arts Ministry
J-3. The Baronial Mansion
J-9. The Jade District Watch House
J-20. The Westside Courthouse
P-11. Customs House

CRIMINAL ORGANIZATIONS

The counterpart to law-enforcement adventures is, of course, criminals. Organized crime in a town like Cat's Cradle can drive many adventures, whether the characters are on the side of good and justice, or are themselves criminals. Criminal-related locations include:

G-10. The Greens (neighborhood)
G-13. The Arcanum (contacts)
G-19. The Warrens (neighborhood and gang)
J-15. The Officers' Club (informal semi-criminal organization)
O-2. The Dogs (point of contact)
O-5. Kennock's Place (major organization)
O-7. Niftin's Knick Knacks (fence)

O-10. Ox's Labor (major figure)
O-17. The Thieves' Guild (major organization)
O-19. The Upper Crust Inn (point of contact)
O-20. Abandoned Tenement (point of contact)
P-6. Dexer's Rooming House (point of contact)

RADICAL POLITICS

Given the current popularity of Baron Scale, radical movements in the town have become less popular and therefore more desperate. A broad variety of radical movements from history can be drawn upon: movements toward democracy, away from democracy, toward or away from religious doctrines of varying kinds, and in favor of rights for groups such as apprentices, students, laborers, or the status of individual professions. The revolt of the Ciompi in Florence and the Gunpowder Plot of 1605 are good examples of this kind of movement.

There is no specific description of any radical movement in the town, but this theme is listed in numerous adventure hooks.
Adventure Hooks: A-9, B-9, C-1, G-3, J-9.

TAVERNS AND INNS

Since the location of a place to stay is often the first question adventurers ask when entering a new city, the following list may save time:

B-1. The Merry Bricklayer
B-14. Barretti's Rooms
D-4. The Sailor's Tavern
G-2. Calibos Inn
G-5. Salt Ale Corner
O-18. Treesa's Pub
O-19. The Upper Crust Inn
P-3. The Calico Cat
P-6. Dexer's Rooming House

MAGICAL RESOURCES AND EQUIPMENT

Cat's Cradle is a major center for alchemy and also contains some spellcasters who might be inclined to buy or sell the odd magic item. Since this is one of the reasons characters tend to gravitate to a city, the following locations can be used as a quick reference if they ask around.

A-3. Ofrenn Vallos Laboratories (alchemical research, not retail)
A-4. Blackstone's Workshop (alchemical research, not retail)
A-5. Guild Lab Facility (point of contact)
A-6. Osenshahle's Lab (alchemical research, not retail)
A-10. Alchemists' Guild House (point of contact)
A-13. Babbson Goold's Laboratory and Alchemical Bazaar (retail)
B-11. Perfumer (specific retail)
G-12. Academy Sales (alchemical)
G-13. The Arcanum (items and supplies)
G-18. Avar's Alchemicals (retail)
J-1. The Alchemists College (point of contact)
J-19. Uiregard's Enchantments (wizard for hire)
J-21. Wythys and Daughter (apothecary)
O-7. Niftin's Knick Knacks (possibly)
O-15. Shevekka's (wizard for hire)
P-8. Alchemical Bazaar (major retail area)

ALCHEMIST'S ALLEY

This pleasant strip of greenery lies along the banks of the narrow Quicksilver River and is officially called the Baronial Corridor. It is most commonly referred to by the general populace as Alchemists' Alley, however, and its location and relative isolation is as much for general safety as any other reason. In the past, alchemical experimentation and manufacture was allowed throughout the city, but a series of minor disasters built to a great catastrophe when a massive explosion and fire destroyed much of the Dockside District a century ago. After this event, alchemical manufacture was limited to the Baronial Corridor, and the river walls were reinforced to protect the rest of the city. Sales of alchemical substances and products remained legal within the city, but the actual creation of alchemicals remains limited to this part of the city, where baronial inspectors can keep a close watch on procedures and issue fines or sanctions if necessary. The entire strip of land is officially baronial territory, and those who work here must lease their space from the barony and agree to abide by strict rules regarding the handling and use of potentially hazardous substances.

A-1. HYON RIVER INLET

As in the Dockside District, the baron's strict safety regulations have not prevented significant alchemical runoff from poisoning nearby waters, turning the Quicksilver River into something of a toxic stew, black and often redolent of bizarre pollutants. Periodic attempts to clean up the mess occur when alchemists and assistants venture into the inlet with various chemicals intended to neutralize the more toxic elements in the water. These efforts are often inadequate, but at least keep the toxicity to a minimum.

Such work is necessary, especially after several incidents in which local fish were adversely affected by the pollution and transformed into savage mutants, some of which waded ashore, killing and causing extensive damage. Some even go so far as to claim that some of the more troublesome river monsters are a result of alchemical mutation from either Dockside or the Quicksilver, a suggestion that most alchemists dispute ferociously.

Adventure Hook: The characters might be hired to hunt river monsters here, chase one down that appears in the Hyon River itself, or even defend the city streets against one that emerges onto the shore.

A-2. SOUTH BRIDGE

The two bridges that arch over the Quicksilver River are sturdy, extensively reinforced, and regularly inspected as they carry traffic between the two parts of the city and pass through the potentially dangerous territory of the Baronial Corridor. Loss of either bridge would represent a significant challenge to the city, so both must remain standing and in good repair. South Bridge is built in the style of the old Gold District, with white stone facing and green slate decorations. It is a relatively plain span, but many feel that it is quite beautiful in its simplicity.

Adventure Hook: Who might use alchemy to blow up a bridge? Bad guys, that's who. Trying to prevent such a plot is an excellent beginning point for an adventure. The Baronial Disaster Brigade, in particular, might be seeking help to uncover such a plot … or infiltrators in the brigade might be the ones behind it. Or both.

A-3. OFRENN VALLOS LABORATORIES

Ofrenn Vallos is a relatively young alchemist noted for his wildly experimental and innovative procedures — procedures that sometimes backfire with dangerous results. Though he has been sanctioned and fined by the barony several times, Vallos continues to pursue various wild avenues of alchemical research in the hope of revolutionizing the entire trade. Realizing that some of his procedures might be troublesome, Vallos has worked with engineers and artisans to isolate his lab space, reinforcing its walls heavily and isolating it from his adjoining living quarters. Vallos also paid premium prices for the installation of an elaborate ventilation and filtration system used in many dwarven forges and designed to keep fresh air circulating and toxic gases to a minimum, thus making his workspace a modern marvel of efficiency.

Despite his brilliance and the sleek modernity of his lab facilities, Vallos has a number of character flaws that prevent him from attaining the fame and notoriety he feels he deserves. Impulsive and often absentminded, Vallos has

been quite lucky in discovering several new formulae, whose sale has kept him solvent. On the other hand, he is indiscriminate in his experimentation, often wasting valuable components on hypothetical formulae that prove to be utter dead-ends. He is also prone to believe rumors and wild stories, and often sends well-paid adventurers on wild goose chases to seek out nonexistent substances or items with exaggerated powers that prove disappointing.

As a consequence, Vallos has grown increasingly desperate for an infusion of funds, though so far he has not taken practical steps to rein in his excessive spending. Instead, he has redoubled his efforts at research and spends late nights at the guild library and elsewhere seeking out information on ancient alchemical secrets and substances, ever searching for forgotten lore that he can use to get himself out of debt. He has so far found some promising leads, but nothing definitive, and is considering using the last of his funds to finance expeditions to seek out rare materials in the hope that they will rescue his slowly sinking business.

Adventure Hook: The characters might be working for Vallos to find ingredients, but a more interesting possibility is that he offers them a share of the profits in a particular idea if they handle the details of putting it into operation. This might include persuading a supplier, negotiating with (or intimidating) criminal elements who are trying to take a cut, or protecting the shipping of a valuable commodity on the river or along a caravan route.

A-4. BLACKSTONE'S WORKSHOP

The premiere gnomish alchemist in Cat's Cradle, **Andreanna Blackstone** maintains living quarters in both the Jade and Gold districts, as well as having an estate outside of town. Her facilities here are thought by many to be utterly chaotic, though Blackstone herself has absolutely no difficulties in navigating the tangle of tubes, glassware, tables, shelves, books, scrolls, bins, jars, and similar objects. To her intensely gnomish mind, the lab is perfectly organized with everything exactly where it needs to be — in fact, she loudly protests any and all attempts to "tidy up" or otherwise alter her work environment by servants, relatives, or well-meaning visitors.

Adventure Hook: An alchemist this rich and prominent is a prime target for kidnapping. The characters might be hired to protect her after her relatives learn of a threat, while a less-morally inclined party might be hired to effect the kidnapping.

A-5. GUILD LAB FACILITY

Not all aspiring alchemists can afford their own manufacturing or experimental facilities, so members of the Alchemists' Guild can rent workspace in this large, dark, brick structure. The main floor is devoted to large rooms with long tables, with glassware, crucibles, ceramics and basic supplies available to all. These larger rooms are communally used by several alchemists at a time who work creating non-volatile compounds. Beneath the main floor are fortified individual work rooms designed to contain any spills or fires. The second floor is devoted to meeting space, a library, and offices for some Alchemical College professors who maintain separate offices here.

Adventure Hook: One of the alchemists renting space in the laboratory is working on a project far more innovative than the normal daily grind, and a rival alchemist has realized it. The only physical copy of the recipe is kept in a lockbox in the lab, and the rival wants the characters to steal it for him.

A-6. OSENSHAHLE'S LAB

This disorderly building serves as the research and manufacturing facility for the increasingly unstable **Osenshahle Warne,** a once-brilliant alchemist whose obsessive personality brought her to the verge of mental collapse. Though she sometimes conducts illegal experiments at her home in Coin City and has let the proud manse degenerate into a ramshackle health hazard, Osenshahle increasingly calls this lab her home. She sleeps on a cot surrounded by bottles and half-eaten food, shambles to her experimental facilities to work, concocts strange alchemicals, and mumbles to herself. She drove off all of her apprentices and servants, and keeping the place in any kind of order proved too much for her easily distracted mind. Other guild alchemists have grown concerned at the lab's safety and cleanliness but so far Osenshahle's influence has kept the barony and inspectors at bay. Some believe it is only a matter of time before the unfortunate alchemist loses touch with reality altogether and causes a terrible catastrophe.

Adventure Hook: The catastrophe takes place, requiring the characters to deal with a situation a bit like a fire spreading into the city, but magical in origin. This might involve rescuing people from buildings, fighting maddened animals, or whatever type of weird catastrophe you care to invent. In this hook, the Baronial Disaster Brigade (**Location A-7**) is a good resource for you to involve.

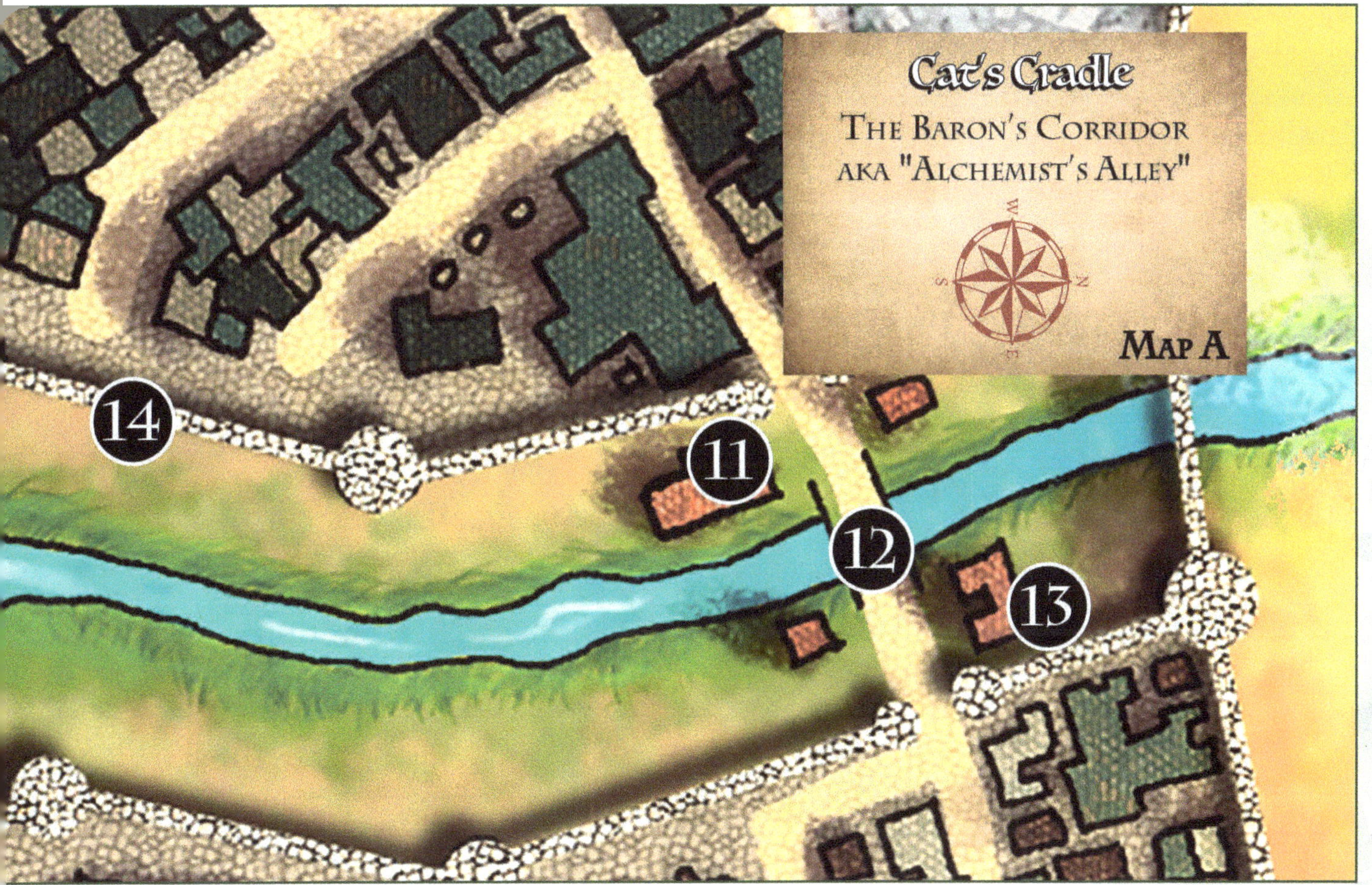

A-7. Baronial Disaster Brigade

Among the measures introduced by the barony in the wake of the Dockside catastrophe a century ago was the creation of a permanent group of disaster specialists who were stationed in the Baronial Corridor, ready to respond to alchemical disasters at a moment's notice. The Baronial Disaster Brigade — or BDB — is an elite group of 12 alchemists, spellcasters, and firefighters equipped with various spells, equipment, and neutralizing agents intended to stop alchemical fires or explosions from spreading or causing further damage. The brigade operates in squads of six, each occupying this squat stone fortress for three-day shifts. The remainder of the brigade, as well as a score of associated volunteers, can be summoned at a few minutes' notice should disaster strike. The brigade is under the command of **Captain Hanrik Kalmester**, a veteran militia officer chosen for his leadership and organizational skills.

Adventure Hook: This is a good group for middle-level characters to join on an ad-hoc basis for an adventure or two, whether it be a catastrophe like the adventure hook in **A-6** or a law enforcement type of plot like the adventure hook in **A-2**. Members of the brigade might be sent to respond to disasters in places other than Cat's Cradle, too, if you want the characters to have the option of traveling a bit.

A-8. Rainbow Grove

This stand of trees is different from the other greenery in the corridor, as it contains trees and plants that were the subject of various alchemical experiments over the years, and continues to be the site of test growths and treatments. Alders cluster near the riverbank, while oak and chestnut grow farther inland. Though many of these trees look entirely natural, a large number have been affected by the various alchemical substances in the soil and now sprout leaves in a myriad of colors, lending the grove its name. Testing by the barony and the alchemists themselves has so far shown that the soil and the trees are relatively harmless, and the grove is a popular destination for picnickers, sightseers, and those who need some isolation from the daily bustle on the streets of Cat's Cradle.

A-9. The Quicksilver

The Quicksilver River is so narrow that it barely merits the name. With effort, alchemists and groundskeepers have kept the corridor itself relatively pleasant and verdant, but the degree of toxicity in the river itself grows greater as it approaches the inlet, where the majority of the pollutants are deposited.

Recently, the level of pollution came to the baron's attention as several small fires actually broke out on the river's surface near where it meets the inlet. Alarmed, the baron decreed that alchemists must reduce the amount of waste emptied into the river through recycling or other forms of disposal lest the trouble spread and cause another massive catastrophe. So far, the decree has met with considerable pushback as alchemists refuse to cooperate, claiming that they are already doing all they can to keep the river safe.

Adventure Hook: Guarding several wagons of toxic waste might seem like an easy task, but certain individuals might have a use for it and attack those wagons. Lower-level characters could be hired as guards and end up in the middle of the city's political network if, for example, the people planning to hijack the wagon are terrorists (or criminals unknowingly working for terrorists). See **Radical Politics** in the Introduction.

A-10. Alchemists' Guild House

The alchemists of Cat's Cradle are a secretive lot, reluctant to share their private formulae and sources. On the other hand, alchemists have few qualms about sharing common techniques and educating students to serve as assistants or bring alchemical procedures to other regions. Both of these tendencies are well displayed by the Alchemists' Guild, a trade organization which all practitioners in Cat's Cradle are required to join in order to do business in the city.

The Guild House is a sturdy, thick-walled villa with numerous meeting rooms, salons, and galleries, as well as an extensive library of common alchemistry knowledge and guest rooms for visiting dignitaries or lecturers. Regular meetings take place at which members set prices, negotiate trade contracts, consult with merchants, and establish general rules for business within the city.

Adventure Hook: The ordinary security force that guards the Guild House suddenly has a rash of a debilitating illness, which is highly uncommon in Cat's Cradle. The characters might be hired to protect the place (because obviously there is something very suspicious going on) or this might even lead them to investigate whether someone is in control of who falls sick and who doesn't.

A-11. Degra Estate

The current master of the Alchemist Guild lives and works in this structure, an older building whose rough fieldstone structure belies its comfortable interior. Walled grounds contain several outbuildings and storage sheds where **Norda Degra** (a half-elven **master alchemist**) performs experiments and formulates extremely potent alchemicals. She specializes in rare and expensive substances that are sold in very small quantities in exclusive sites throughout Cat's Cradle. These substances include poison antidotes, healing salves, substances that enhance Intelligence, Charisma, and other abilities, rejuvenation tinctures, substances that improve spellcasting abilities, and the like. A skilled and experienced practitioner, Degra is also a highly law-abiding and loyal citizen who favors working with non-volatile and less harmful substances, and always makes certain to dispose of alchemical waste safely as per baronial decree. As a prosperous, successful, and lawful alchemist, she was a natural choice to lead the guild and has held the position through yearly elections for nearly a decade.

Degra works alone and has no immediate family but is aided by a number of students and servants. Her reputation remains spotless, and she has always made it clear that she does not create harmful or destructive substances such as poisons or explosives.

Adventure Hook: Degra remains above suspicion, but unfortunately a carefully concealed past has finally returned to haunt her, and she has been drawn against her will into a dark conspiracy that could shake Cat's Cradle to its foundations (see **Cat's Cradle: Fortune Hunters** for more details).

A-12. Count Mustaf Bridge

The northernmost bridge across the Hyon River is on the site of the oldest bridge in Cat's Cradle. Originally a wooden span intended to connect both sides of the growing settlement, the bridge was replaced by a fine gray stone structure funded by the civic-minded Count Mustaf more than 100 years ago. Mustaf hired well-known artisans and dwarven engineers for the project, and they succeeded spectacularly, creating an enduring structure that has survived decades of heavy use and traffic. So well-constructed is the bridge that no seams can be detected between stones, and the decorative carvings — the blazons of the city of Cat's Cradle, Count Mustaf, and the barony itself — are as sharp and clear as they were the day they were carved.

A-13. Babbson Goold's Laboratory and Alchemical Bazaar

Owing to its convenient location close to the Mustaf Bridge, Goold's alchemical store is the best-known and most-visited such location in the city. **Babbson Goold** himself is a portly, companionable man with a ready laugh and a charming manner, but at the same time he is a skilled businessman who knows how to turn a profit. His unerring instincts tell him when to negotiate, when to stand firm, and exactly what prices the market will bear, characteristics that have been variously described as "uncanny," "supernatural," and "kind of creepy, really."

The bazaar is considered to be quite an exciting place to shop, as the shelves are crowded with alchemicals of all description, and Goold's "secret bargains" are hidden throughout the establishment, awaiting discovery by careful shoppers. All of the shelves are locked and secured behind alchemically enhanced glass, accessible only by Goold's army of halfling and gnome assistants, who are all friendly and well-informed, with a seemingly bottomless store of knowledge about the bazaar and its wares.

Adventure Hook: Goold hires the characters to investigate and provide security for the purchase of a large quantity of alchemical supplies shipped in from outside the town. This is highly suspicious, as Cat's Cradle is by far the best source of such materials and exports rather than imports them.

A-14. Westriver Wall

Flanking the Hyon, the Westriver Wall is twin to its eastside cousin, similarly white and carefully tended, with extra stone cladding added to help protect the luxurious buildings of the Jade District from any potential hazard originating in Alchemists' Alley. As it stands guard over the city's wealthiest neighborhood, it is regularly patrolled and its towers are well garrisoned by the watch, despite the fact that the entire area is virtually crime-free.

BRICKTOWN

Bricktown is the city's main non-alchemical industrial district.

Most of the buildings here are constructed from the dark red brick for which Cat's Cradle is famous. The widespread use of bricks in the district spared it from much of the devastation wrecked by the mass erosion of ripplestone a hundred years ago, and the subsequent expansion gave the district its common name. Today, brick ovens, glass furnaces, and forges found throughout the neighborhood contribute to the area's famed heat, which makes some streets all but uninhabitable in summer, but which also provide enough warmth in winter to draw the homeless and the poor from all across Cat's Cradle.

The ready availability of forges, ovens, and furnaces makes the area a potent draw for artisans as well, though competition for space is intense and only the most successful or influential of artists can afford to live or work here. Younger and less prominent artisans must make their way in the Old City where housing and work space come less dearly.

B-1. THE MERRY BRICKLAYER

The premiere tavern of Bricktown region, the Merry Bricklayer is operated by the graying innkeeper **Davril Haegeson** and his family. The tavern comes by its name honestly, for Davril is indeed a retired bricklayer and -maker who carefully husbanded his fees and salary over decades to realize his dream of owning his very own tavern. For over a decade now, Davril has run a warm, comfortable, and popular business, surviving various economic ups and downs as well as the tragic death of his wife three years ago, but his health is beginning to fail and even his seemingly endless optimism and good nature has begun to flag. Several enterprising individuals have expressed interest in buying the tavern, the most prominent of which is Gellor Trendar, owner of Mystic Stone, who has made an extremely generous offer. Trendar hopes to open a series of Merry Bricklayer taverns across Cat's Cradle and beyond, under his ownership but managed by his employees. So far, Davril has resisted efforts to purchase the tavern, proclaiming that he would rather die behind the bar. His six children have responded to this in a variety of ways. Daughters **Hildra** and **Edyth** love their father with all their hearts and support him, while eldest son **Sorvan** and eldest daughter **Sylea** both profess affection for Davril and urge him to retire in comfort on the proceeds of the sale, but have allowed that he has a right to choose his own future. Davril's youngest sons **Thravan** and **Kendro** claim to go along with their older siblings in allowing their father to make his own choices, but in reality they desperately lust after the fortune in gold offered by Gellor, which they will share in should their father agree. They have both undertaken an intense campaign to persuade Sorvan and Sylea, or at least one of them, as the eldest siblings will eventually inherit the tavern, and can sell out after their father is conveniently out of the way.

Adventure Hook: Thravan and Kendro are not terribly patient about the situation, however, for both have been living fairly lavish lifestyles and are badly in debt. Should Sorvan and Sylea agree to sell the tavern if they inherit, the younger brothers may take matters into their own hands and hasten their father's demise.

B-2. BELLSINGER GOLDSMITH

Gnomish goldsmith **Studi Bellsinger** operates a small, spotless, and exquisitely organized shop. Here she creates jewelry in many styles, using casting and handcrafting techniques. Her more expensive pieces are magically enhanced by Studi's cousin, the illusionist **Agno** who provides improvements ranging from aesthetic alterations to protective magic. Studi herself is as professional buttoned-down as her shop, with a spotless reputation for honesty and skill.

Studi's best qualities — her talent and organization — actually make her a target for the most cunning of criminals. In order to remain on schedule and provide her clients' jewelry promptly, Studi keeps a fortune in gems, magical components, gold, silver, and other precious metals close at hand, secured in a vault located in the back of her shop, adjacent to her small but efficient workshop. Needless to say, this attracts the attention of would-be thieves from all across Cat's Cradle and beyond. The professional criminals of the Kennock Syndicate and the Thieves' Guild have taken a special interest in Studi's shop and facilities and dispatched several of their most talented operatives to break in and make off with the contents of her vault.

Unfortunately, Studi proved every bit as devious as her opponents, and so far, none has succeeded in their endeavors. Despite its rather mundane appearance, her shop is a nightmarish labyrinth of locks, traps and pitfalls that she activates during hours that the shop is closed, and that she can also

BRICKMAKING

While obviously volumes could be (and have been) devoted to the history and manufacture of bricks, knowing the basics helps understand Bricktown and its primary industry. Though it plays a subordinate role to Cat's Cradle's more glamorous and profitable industries — alchemical salts and their associated endeavors — brickmaking is an important cornerstone of the city's economy, one which is not dependent upon the vagaries of magic and the dangers of alchemical manufacture.

Bricks are composed primarily of clay and sand or shale, with various other materials added to provide coloration and durability. Each of Cat's Cradle's major brick manufacturers has its own closely guarded special formula, and the bricks have their own unique qualities. The sand and clay mixture is packed into wooden molds by hand, then dried for several days and fired in a specially designed kiln, first at low heat to remove remaining moisture, then at higher temperatures to fire and strengthen the brick. Finished bricks are stored either in attached warehouses or at the Brickfield, a large facility maintained by the barony, where local manufacturers can store their bricks for a fee prior to transportation.

Cat's Cradle's location along the shores of a major lake provide brickmakers with distinct advantages — clay, shale, and sand are readily available and can be quickly transported to the city's various brickyards. Bricks originating in Cat's Cradle have been used across the continent and have a reputation for beauty and quality, which leads to fierce competition among manufacturers, and in some cases outright industrial sabotage.

call upon should anyone attempt a daylight robbery (so far no one has, but she is prepared nonetheless). Studi, Agno, and other members of the gnomish community designed these traps, and they are deadly, difficult to locate, and all but impossible to disarm. Even if intruders miraculously manage to avoid the various spiked pits, swinging guillotines, hidden spears, poison darts, falling blocks, and other obstacles, they will still be confronted by a series of locks and vaults to reach Studi's storage, each one more difficult and elaborate than the last. As noted, no thieves have every been able to circumvent Studi's traps and locks, leading the Kennock Syndicate to contemplate other ways of reaching their goal, including bribing Studi's staff or even attempting to magically control Studi so that she herself disables all of the vault's defenses. Like their other schemes, these have all led to utter failure, but the Syndicate feels that the subtle approach may hold more promise than a direct assault.

Adventure Hook: Studi is incapacitated by an accident, which suddenly renders the entire shop completely inaccessible. A patron who legitimately and legally needs something from the shop hires the characters to do the impossible: break in.

B-3. DWARVEN BRICKWORKS

Despite its name, Dwarven Brickworks is actually controlled by a coalition of dwarves and gnomes who pool their resources — dwarven craftsmanship and gnomish innovation — to construct a fully mechanical factory where bricks and decorative stonework are created without the need for manual labor beyond maintenance of machines.

The Brickworks are housed in a squat, ugly building that constantly belches steam and smoke, emits loud clanking mechanical noises, and hosts a constant stream of wagons and dray animals. Inside is a labyrinth of gears, hydraulics, pistons, conveyor belts, bins, vats, ovens, and other gear, some of which simply defies description or understanding.

The dwarves of Clan Forgefire control the dwarven side of the business, which involves the crafting of the various machines, their construction and maintenance, while gnomes from a variety of different families and backgrounds take care of the design and creative side, constantly concocting new devices and manufacturing processes, designing new brick shapes, glazes and appearances, and experimenting with various formulations seeking to improve on their old designs.

Some of the time, of course, this unrestricted experimentation and chaos results in spectacular failure — explosions, fires, noxious gases, and malfunctioning

BROKN THUMB
Sticks and Bricks Road
Artisan's Walk
Dancer's Road
Ironcart Way
Scruffian St.
Wheedler St.
Gall St.
Seven Macfcall
Rivergate
Statue Street
Tale's Twist
Cat's Cradle
BRICKTOWN
N
W
E
S
MAP B

machinery are all part of daily life at Dwarven Brickworks. A recent attempt to simulate handcrafted quality through the use of clockwork laborers resulted in the devices running wild and damaging several neighboring structures along Sticks-and-Bricks Avenue and costing Clan Forgefire several thousand gold pieces in fines. In another incident, much of the structure was flooded with soft mud when an extrusion device malfunctioned. Such events are taken in stride by the pragmatic dwarves and basically ignored by the gnomes, who continue to dream up wild and often utterly impractical inventions.

Stonelord **Uli Forgefire** is the senior dwarf in attendance, managing his side of the business with considerable acumen and all the wisdom of his 120 years. His gnomish opposite number is the wild-haired **Nika "Gadget" Gemdelver**, a spellcaster who oversees the gnomes primarily because she has the most elaborate and impractical ideas of all her people. Bright and friendly, Nika nevertheless never met an invention she didn't love and must rely on Uli's more pragmatic and sensible leadership to keep her from utterly bankrupting the business.

The Dwarven Brickworks maintains good or at least neutral relations with the other brick manufacturers, conducting business cordially while dealing firmly with attempts at industrial espionage. In general, they are left out of major conflicts between businesses since their purely mechanical process is considered either utterly mad or prohibitively expensive. All the same, grim Forgefire dwarves guard the facility and keep out unwanted visitors, while the gnomes happily conduct official tours of the facilities for the curious.

Like many locations in Bricktown, the vicinity of Dwarven Brickworks is hot and often humid due to the moisture extracted from drying bricks. The dwarves and gnomes are sturdy and tolerate these conditions without much difficulty, but humans and elves often find it uncomfortable, especially in the heat of summer. Also like other businesses in Bricktown, Dwarven Brickworks attracts crowds of homeless cityfolk during the coldest days of winter. Despite a gruff character, Uli tolerates these transients and often provides them with food and clothing.

Adventure Hook: A building site in the town keeps getting sabotaged. Uli and Nika only happen to know about it because they are the suppliers for the construction team, but they can refer the characters to a building contractor who is at his wits' end trying to find out what is happening to the job and why.

B-4. The Brickfield

Officially baronial territory, the Brickfield is a vast warehouse where finished bricks can be stored prior to transportation. Storage is in short supply, but the warehouse has grown more vital as production increases. Space must be reserved weeks or even months in advance, and though fees for the service are relatively low, they must all be fully paid to the barony in advance. Should misfortune delay a shipment, penalties of up to 100% of the advance fees may be imposed. Worse still, should a customer fail to remove their bricks on schedule — thus delaying the space's next occupants — the baron reserves the right to confiscate and sell the offending bricks. In such cases, the customers usually move the bricks out of the warehouse with great urgency.

Due to its importance to the city and the barony, the Brickfield is built like a fortress with thick walls (of Cat's Cradle brick, naturally), secure gates, and narrow windows. A single set of large gates is kept barred save for when shipments are coming in or going out. Well-trained and well-paid guards maintain security, often supplemented by spellcasters. Those trusted with this task are invariably above suspicion and considered all but uncorruptible. Despite this, intrigue and sabotage sometimes occur, with bricks stolen and damaged or buyers paid off to cancel their shipments at the last minute to guarantee forfeiture. The Brickfield's overseer is the tough and no-nonsense veteran **Colonel Grif Nishon**, who tolerates neither slacking, dishonesty, nor disobedience, and is unflaggingly loyal to the baron.

B-5. Black Bull Ironworks

Urthan "The Bull" Viturri is a human barbarian from a distant land (he has never confided exactly which one) who is a master blacksmith and has gained sufficient success and influence to obtain a small but well-equipped smithy in the heart of Bricktown. There he makes mundane objects such as pots, kettles, and utensils, but also crafts especially fine weapons and armor for special clients. These items are often intended for enchantment and a future as magic items, and so are created with the highest standards of quality and beauty. Urthan is assisted by his two wives, **Shan** and **Khur**, who are every bit as tough and skilled as he is, and his four children. The family lives in a suite of apartments above the smithy.

Quiet, morose, and often downright surly, Urthan nonetheless commands high prices for his work, and many of his wares decorate noble mansions or are worn and carried into battle by wealthy warriors. Despite his success, some dark rumors have continued to persist about Urthan, many of which surround his reasons for leaving his homeland. Perhaps this is simply due to his reluctance to discuss it, but wild stories circulate nonetheless — some claim that he came to Cat's Cradle after committing a terrible crime, that he was once a powerful warlord toppled from his throne by rebellion and that the rebels are still seeking him, that he secretly worships foreign gods and makes sacrifice to them while using his victims' blood to make his various wares — these and even more bizarre stories have been whispered about Urthan. The Bull himself doesn't deign to respond to these rumors, and most are far too scared of what he might do to actually bring up any of them directly. In some ways, the rumors have enhanced Urthan's reputation and business, for more people have begun to stop by simply to see him in the flesh.

Adventure Hook: Someone has learned a secret from Urthan's past and is trying to blackmail him. Urthan realizes he doesn't have the social cunning required to trap such a villain and enlists the characters to help.

B-6. Whiteshadow Ceramics

Deera Whiteshadow is from a family of halfling craftsfolk and has taken to her clan's mastery of stoneware and porcelain. When her brothers and sisters chose to remain in their family's home territory, she set out on her own, venturing to Cat's Cradle, where she bought a bankrupt brickworks and converted it to the production of ceramics. Using similar techniques to brickmaking, Deera was able to piggyback on Cat's Cradle's supply chain, importing the clays and glazes she needed to create and improve upon her family's traditional wares. Today, her facilities are staffed primarily by halflings and gnomes and are entirely self-contained, including storage, workshops, kilns, and warehouse space. Whiteshadow stoneware is durable and inexpensive and is balanced by Whiteshadow porcelain, which is prized for its beauty, texture, and fine glazes. Patterns incorporate traditional halfling designs integrated with symbology from other cultures such as elves, humans, and dwarves.

Deera has employed a number of relatives as well. She has never married and has no children of her own and treats the cousins, nieces, and nephews in her employ with near-maternal concern and care. Though she claims to love them all equally, it is clear that her favorite is her nephew, the young Nardo Brooks, a young and brash halfling who plays his aunt's affections for all they're worth. Gambling, carousing, indiscriminately pursuing romantic assignations, brawling, and sampling as many exotic substances as possible, Nardo is anything but the paragon of halfling virtue that Deera thinks he is. For her part, Deera refuses to hear anything negative about her nephew, assuming that others are simply jealous, and bails him out with no questions asked whenever his excesses get him locked up. Her warm relations with powerful businesses and city officials are usually enough to get major charges dismissed or to get young Nardo out with a slap on the wrist. It is rumored that Nardo is deeply in debt to the Kennock Syndicate, who are attempting to blackmail him into embezzling from Deera or into skimming off the top of Whiteshadow porcelain shipments. Time will tell whether he finally betrays his aunt, though even then she may find a way to forgive him.

Adventure Hook: Deera hires the characters to investigate Nardo's activities and keep him out of trouble.

B-7. Manticore Bricks

One of the three leading brick manufacturers in Cat's Cradle, Manticore takes pride in its "all natural" production methods, which the current owner **Mikelos Creal** insists is made with no mechanical or magical enhancement whatsoever. Manticore's success lies in its variety, as its bricks are valued for their many colors, shapes, styles, and levels of quality and aesthetic value, ranging from common bricks used for basic construction to elaborate, fanciful bricks with delicate embossing or patterns and brightly colored glazed stones that are greatly prized and incorporated into many famed structures and luxurious homes in distant regions.

As might be expected, other manufacturers offer significant rewards for the various formulae and processes that Manticore uses, particularly the arcanists at Mystic Stone (**Location B-9**), who are baffled by Manticore's success and their rejection of magical enhancement. Crea and his partners are aware of Mystic's activities and hired their own spellcasters (at significant expense) to protect Manticore's operation. This has led to occasional outright confrontations, and even a full-scale spell battle in the facility when magically concealed rogues and their sorcerer supervisor were discovered sneaking into the Manticore facility. Rumor has it that Manticore's owners are furious about the intrusion and have been planning some form of retaliation.

Much to the frustration of Mystic Stone and many other local manufacturers, Manticore has been awarded an official baronial contract to produce bricks in a planned urban renewal project, replacing the unstable ripplestone structures of the Old City with sturdy, locally produced brickwork. The plan is still in its infancy and years from completion, but Mikelos and his associates have already begun planning for the ambitious endeavor.

Adventure Hook: The owners of Mystic Stone (**Location B-9**) hire — or attempt to hire — the characters to steal the formula from Mikelos. If the characters choose not to engage in such nefarious behavior, the scenario can turn around. If informed of the plot, Mikelos hires them to protect the formula from whomever Mystic Stone hires next. The same hook could be used for attempted sabotage of the baronial contract.

B-8. Milleton Glassworks

One of the various businesses not directly related to brick manufacture, the Glassworks also features massive furnaces where a mixture of sand and ash are melted together, sometimes with chemicals to provide color, blown and flattened into panels that grace nobles' homes or temple windows. Glass requires significantly higher temperatures than bricks, so these furnaces are especially hot, making much of the building's interior quite uncomfortable and forcing workers to take short shifts working the furnaces, spending the remainder of their time in other portions of the complex where they pack, organize, and prepare glass for shipment.

From time to time, Milleton employs spellcasters to aid in the glassmaking process by providing magical flames that temporarily increase the efficiency of the glass furnaces, enchanting finished glass objects, or otherwise enhancing the final product.

The Milleton family has run the glassworks for more than 60 years under the control of matriarch **Landra Milleton** who is now 95 years old and (at least in the view of her potential heirs) stubbornly refuses to die. The Milleton Estate (**Location S-7**) is currently a den of intrigue, backstabbing, and competition for the aging family elder's favor by her relatives, children, and even grandchildren.

Adventure Hook: One of the Milleton family factions enlists the characters to strengthen their status. This might happen before Landra dies, or it might be the result of an all-out power struggle just after she dies.

B-9. Mystic Stone

Asea Rohlind (Location G-15) is a half-elven sorceress rejected by her elven family due to her mixed heritage. Bitter but determined, she made her way in human society, discovering her sorcerous gifts along the way and eventually marrying the hard-nosed but entirely nonmagical human merchant **Gellor Trendar** who owned a small brick and ceramics business and had just begun to export his wares outside Cat's Cradle. In time, the two developed new alchemical formulae and adapted techniques normally used in the creation of magical items to strengthen, enhance, and beautify Gellor's products. They also took full advantage of their location, adding some of Cat's Cradle's unique alchemic salts to their mixtures. Soon their bricks gained a stellar reputation and became something of a prestige item for building. Today, Asea and her staff of influential and well-compensated spellcasters continue the tradition, applying their skills to produce bricks of exceptional durability and beauty.

Mystic Stone is the most famous and influential of Cat's Cradle's many brickmakers, but due to the high cost and elaborate procedures needed to make their product, they are not the most prosperous — this honor goes to Mystic Stone's rival, Manticore Bricks, a situation that vexes Asea and Gellor to no end. Their elven wizards and human warlock staff are a generally haughty and arrogant lot in the best of times, and the notion that a mere human business that does not even use magic might be outcompeting them has placed a huge chip on the spellcasters' shoulders. Intrigue against Manticore has been increasing of late, as Asea, Gellor, and their employees seek to learn more about the rival business' secret formulae and procedures.

In addition to the business's two owners, Mystic Stone's senior staff includes four elven wizards — whose versatile spellcasting allows them to experiment with more and different arcane procedures — and two human warlocks. Staff is mostly human with several dwarf laborers. The building has been extensively converted and beautified with brick facing that puts many of the enterprise's most colorful bricks on display, as well as some of their more exotic types, such as bricks that emit light, change shape and color, and other intriguing effects. The interior does not look like a typical brickyard, for the various spellcasters have their own private workspaces, and the actual manufacturing facilities are equipped with magically fueled ovens. Basic labor is performed by unseen servants, and various familiars such as imps and homunculi dart here and there. Bound elementals and even more bizarre and exotic sights are common.

Unlike the tough but kindhearted Uli Forgefire (**Location B-3**), Asea, Gellor, and their spellcasters have little tolerance for loiterers and the poor who venture to Bricktown in the winter to seek out the warmth of the furnaces and kilns. Being the type that sees poverty as a sign of moral weakness and laziness, Mystic Stone's owners employ local toughs to beat and drive off anyone foolish enough to camp or linger too long in the area or anyone who looks shiftless or poverty-stricken.

Adventure Hook: See **Location B-7**. A lower-level adventure hook might be defending some squatters from the thugs employed here, possibly at the urging of a cleric or as part of a radical politics type of campaign.

B-10. SALAMARIS' STUDIO

Eris Salamaris is a human artist who crafts delicate works in ceramic, glass, clay, and metal. His success with the wealthy folk of Cat's Cradle allowed him to renovate a small factory, installing resources for firing ceramics and smelting glass as well as living quarters. Here, Salamaris creates wild and increasingly elaborate works that many feel resemble organically grown objects or bizarre sea life. His works are popular with the elite of Cat's Cradle, and the baron himself recently commissioned a large sculpture that will grace one of the feast halls in Cat's Keep. Salamaris has taken on the project with enthusiasm to the point of obsession, neglecting other projects and commissions in his zeal.

Salamaris' obsession is fed by his dreams, in which he envisions the final shape of his sculpture, which evolves and grows even more elaborate with each dream. Always somewhat unstable, Salamaris has grown more so recently as his consumption of hallucinogens (fairly high to begin with) has increased significantly, providing him with even greater inspiration and the madness that accompanies it. He has driven away most of his assistants, and his studio has gone from pristine good order to utter chaos. Salamaris' wife Azrati has also moved out and is now living in a small apartment. She has sought help for her unfortunate husband and suspects there is more to his malady than simple artistic obsession.

Adventure Hook: There is indeed something unusual about Eris' obsession, which could involve a night hag, demonic possession of some kind, or contact with an elder being. Azrati hires the characters to investigate the situation and resolve it.

B-11. PERFUMER

A mysterious immigrant to Cat's Cradle who is rumored to have significant magical powers, the elf **Ellea Macaethan** owns and operates this shop where she sells perfumes, candles, and essential oils of all varieties, including some that actually have arcane qualities. While most of these effects are minor, benign, and temporary — relaxation, pleasant hallucinations, the enhancement of the senses or feelings of love and pleasure — she also offers more potent items that have effects similar to some magical potions, incenses, and salves. Her manufacturing process is not known — Ellea's shop contains only finished products and modest living quarters, leading most to assume that she has a workspace somewhere outside of Cat's Cradle, possibly in the countryside somewhere or, as some more exotic theories suggest, on a convenient parallel plane or pocket dimension.

Adventure Hook: Ellea has access to a pocket plane she inherited, which she uses as her workroom. However, it has become unstable on the inside for unknown reasons. Ellea isn't an expert in this area, but she knows enough to hire them in situations like this. The characters would need to enter the small plane of existence and explore it to find out where things have gone wrong … and why.

B-12. THE DANCER'S DOOR

Originally known as the Eastern Gate, this entrance to Cat's Cradle sees a constant flow of traffic along Sundry Road, bearing raw materials to Bricktown or carrying loads of finished brick out. As the industry grew in income and importance, the significance of the gate grew until it was decorated with dancing statues and faced with bricks from a variety of manufacturers, making its surface a chaotic mix of bricks in a wide range of shades and colors.

B-13. STURT'S APOTHECARY

Sturt is a jumpy, talkative, and easily distracted shopkeeper, but his wares — healing herbs, salves, medicinal ointments, and related items — are considered top-quality and are especially popular with adventurers. Sturt himself is an expatriate goblin who came to Cat's Cradle along with several of his fellow goblins and a trove of herbalism and formulae stolen from his tribe's shamans. Armed with their pilfered knowledge, Sturt and his friends started selling in the Alchemical Bazaar in the Panhandle, then used their profits to renovate a rundown apothecary in Bricktown where their business has continued to grow.

Adventure Hook: Though Sturt is outwardly a chaotic and unfocused individual, he has proven quite the skilled craftsman, and is a surprisingly cunning and thoughtful individual. He knows, for example, that his tribal shamans do not view his crimes lightly, and may one day seek him out to avenge themselves and eliminate the threat that he represents to their power. Accordingly, he is always on the lookout for suspicious individuals — goblins or otherwise — and is not above soliciting some of his adventurer customers to act as his agents or bodyguards.

B-14. BARRETTI'S ROOMS

A typical Bricktown tenement located close by the Old City, Barretti's is constructed of unstable ripplestone that has been patched over the years with cheap local bricks. Rooms are cheap, and there is always the danger of collapse due to its outdated building materials. The building's most notable tenant is the private detective **Valdrin Hoff** (see *Fortune Hunters*), who maintains a home-office on the ground floor. Here, he meets with clients, researches his various cases, and even consults in great secrecy with various members of the constabulary.

Cat's Keep

Deep in the heart of Cat's Cradle stand the high walls of the baronial keep. Centuries old, the keep is by far the oldest, still-standing structure in the region, predating the discovery of all the more unique aspects of Cat's Cradle and its surrounding environs.

The walls and the keep itself are of simple construction in an ancient style, though the inner castle has been expanded over the centuries in the name of comfort. As was traditional for the region in those ancient days, all local grain was stored inside the keep for safety and fair distribution, so most of the outbuildings between the little castle and the keep wall are warehouses and silos for storage of common-use dry goods.

By tradition, the keep is also home to a large population of domestic and semi-feral cats. These are fed out of the baronial budget and serve as guardians of the grain stores against pests.

C-1. The Baronial Castle

The largest and oldest of the keep's inner buildings is the Baronial Castle. Simpler and more down to earth than the extravagant homes of the Jade District, this castle is one reason Baron Scale is well-regarded by his people. He is the first baron in three generations to live full time in the castle, instead of showing up at the keep only for major events while living in the Jade District.

By tradition, petitions from the common people are heard once a week in the castle's front audience chamber, which is well-appointed but far from ostentatious. Baron Scale, Baroness Liera, and their two small children are all said to be gracious hosts, able to make anyone, from the highest noble to the lowliest commoner, feel comfortable in their home. The baron's mother, Lady Resla, has a more forbidding reputation, and her quarters in the castle are said to be far more reminiscent of the last few generations' opulence.

Adventure Hook: This area will likely be used if the baron or one of the nobility hires the characters for an adventure, but the possibility of problems at the weekly audience can be a good independent hook since the baron himself is usually present. This is most likely a radical political sort of plot that could range from something as minor as a protest to something as serious as an assassination attempt.

C-2. The Baronial Stables

The baronial stables stand at the back of the keep, far from the gate, and — secured as they are behind the keep's high walls — are considered some of the best-protected stables in the land. These were built centuries ago by one of the baron's ancestors and are of little interest to Baron Scale. He keeps only a few horses for himself and his family, of quality but hardly theft-worthy stock — especially considering how many easier places there are from which to steal horses.

That said, other wealthy and important people do sometimes want a secure location to house a valuable horse, and the baronial stables are a highly sought-after space for the keeping of prime grade mounts. As many as 10 to 15 expensive horses can be found housed alongside those of the baron, enough to have inspired several attempts on the place, but thus far, no would-be horse thieves have succeeded at stealing from the baronial stables.

Adventure Hook: A character's horse is stolen and ends up at the baronial stables. Obviously the most sensible way to deal with this is to steal it back, right?

C-3. The Baronial Temple

The oldest still-standing temple in the Cat's Cradle region is the baronial temple inside the walls of Cat's Keep. Small and simple in structure, the temple is dedicated to two deities. By her statue's symbolism, one is clearly identifiable as Sefagreth, the god of trade who is revered throughout the city, but the other statue, known only as the "Bearded God," is unidentifiable and a mystery. Every few generations, the bearded god takes on a different identity and significance for the common people of Cat's Cradle, who are permitted to visit the baronial temple a few times a year on major holidays.

It is said, however, that the baron's family knows the true identity of the bearded god, and that they worship him in secret rites to keep Cat's Cradle safe and the baronial family in power from generation to generation. The baronial family and the temple priest have always insisted that all worship taking place at the baronial temple is perfectly normal, and they never argue with the public as to the bearded god's currently accepted identity.

Despite the simplicity of this ancient temple and its central statues, everything else in the temple is dripping with gold, gems, and silk, and as such, is heavily guarded. Offerings at this temple are all in coin by tradition, and as temple expenses are paid by the baron, said offerings are distributed among the poor once a year at the winter festival.

C-4. The City Courthouse

Opposite the watch house, just inside the keep gate, stands the Cat's Cradle Courthouse. Here, the baron's appointed judges weigh all legal matters from atop a rather intimidating dais. The courthouse is not large, but most of it is a single, echoing hall with a high ceiling and very few furnishings.

Accusers and accused, criminals and watch members stand below the dais to make their cases, only rarely represented by legal advocates or accompanied by supporters or corroborators. Court guards, not members of the watch, maintain safety and order when plaintiffs or defendants are unruly. A small number of benches allow for an audience, but most cases are observed only by one of the baron's secretaries who keeps verbatim notes of each case. There is no place for anything remotely like a jury in this courthouse. Everything is up to the judge.

While some difficult or high-profile cases are referred directly to the baron, and while it is technically possible to appeal to the baron for reversal of judgments in any legal matter, the majority of legal and criminal matters are decided here (and most petitions for appeal are rejected, as the baron is kept very busy running the city and surrounding countryside). Fortunately, the baron's three appointed judges are all known to be wise, even-tempered, shrewd, and compassionate individuals.

Senna Tyhrese is an old elf woman who has lived in these lands for hundreds of years. **Tonsren Weckam** is a human elder and lifelong philanthropist. **Kyrissa Dess** is a yshkat woman who formerly worked as a mediator at the docks, solving disputes between merchants and captains. All three are experts in local and kingdom law, and though all are very minor aristocrats, all seem sympathetic to the plight of common folk. Obviously, they cannot try cases for citizens who outrank them (the rank of a baron-appointed judge in Cat's Cradle being considered equal to that of baronet), and residents and visitors who outrank a baron must take their cases before their own or the baron's liege.

Adventure Hook: The characters are called upon to gather evidence in a case where nothing seems well established. If they are unwittingly on the trail of someone powerful, they might rapidly become the victims of a second crime.

C-5. The Groundskeeper's Shed

Located just behind the castle and entirely dwarfed by it stands a groundskeeper's shed as large as some families' entire homes. While it does contain the tools one would expect for gardeners to maintain the flowerbeds inside Cat's Keep, it has long been tradition for the groundskeepers to also care for Cat's Keep's army of cats. As such, more than half the shed is dedicated to veterinary care and other necessary tools for the sanitary accommodation of so many felines.

The Cat's Keep grounds are kept very clean but still tend to smell a bit like cat, especially on hot days.

C-6. The Guest House

Built centuries ago by a previous baroness, the structure now known as the Guest House was originally for her second husband and his art projects, while the first husband lived in the castle as her official consort. Later, this "Second House" came to be used for important guests to Cat's Cradle whenever there wasn't room in the castle. In recent generations, after Baron Scolren moved his family to the Jade District, the guest house was shut up and went unused for decades.

Since Baron Scale returned to Cat's Keep, however, the Guest House has been renovated and is said to be very fine, perhaps more comfortable than the castle itself.

Adventure Hook: Unexpected and important guests are arriving with virtually no notice. The characters are employed to augment the normal security that would be employed in this case, possibly because there are suspicions that corrupt elements in the city watch have been paid to let their attention lapse at a key moment.

C–7. The Inner Gates

Also known as the Old Gates, these are the gates to Cat's Keep. Something truly terrible and unexpected would have to happen in Cat's Cradle for the Keep Gates to be of any practical use, so these days they are left open night and day, closed only briefly as part of seasonal holiday traditions, such as preceding all observances surrounding the Main Silo (**Location C-8**). That said, the gates are guarded by the watch, as they are right beside the central watch house and courthouse. And since they are used ceremonially a few times a year, they are kept in reasonably good repair, especially the hinges and the portcullis chain.

Though the portcullis is sturdy steel and the gates themselves quite stout and steel-reinforced, it is unknown whether they could still withstand an assault by an enemy force, since their construction predates several advancements in siege weaponry. They do look imposing, however. The gates would almost certainly be able to keep out rioting peasants at the very least, though Baron Scale and his family are quite popular, and riots in Cat's Cradle seem unlikely for now.

C–8. The Main Silo

Most of the buildings inside Cat's Keep are used to store grain and other long-term food supplies. It's just the Cat's Cradle tradition, and no one has ever seen fit to change it. Obviously, many merchants handle their own storage, but small-time farmers can rarely find a better deal than to sell their surplus to the baron for distribution, especially with a baron like Scale, who pays a fair price even to commoners. In addition, Cat's Cradle still allows the payment of taxes in kind, so most small-time farmers (which describes most of those who work the baron's lands) find it easiest to pay the baron in the fruits of their labors. As

such, the so-called "Main Silo" is actually among the smallest of Cat's Keep's food storage structures.

However, the Main Silo is the oldest of these, and of great cultural importance. Decorated top to bottom with carvings depicting the city's history, the Cat's Keep Main Silo is the most prominent feature of the keep's front courtyard. Every year at harvest time, a ritual is made of mixing together wheat from everyone's harvests to symbolize the unity of the Cat's Cradle community. On the winter's shortest day, bags of wheat from the Main Silo are ritually distributed to those in need. If any is left over come spring, farmers who work the baron's lands are given sacks of wheat at a planting ritual as a symbol of the cycle of giving and receiving in a community.

If harm were to come to the Cat's Keep Main Silo, it would not be a particular financial loss to anyone, and in most years no one would likely go hungry either. However, the loss of the Main Silo's grain would strike a deep blow to community morale. Of course, the Main Silo stands directly between the castle and the central watch house, in plain view of anyone passing by, so it would be all but impossible to tamper with it without getting caught.

C–9. The Tower

Cat's Cradle may be a wealthy city, but it is still only a barony, and as such has no authority to imprison anyone provably ranked baron or higher without orders from the capital. However, on occasion, a person of great wealth or renown, or who *might* be nobility but is waiting for proof to arrive, needs to be arrested for criminal behavior. In such a case, it is considered inappropriate to house such a person with common prisoners unless absolutely no alternative is available.

In Cat's Cradle, so long as a high-status prisoner is not deemed a personal threat to the baron, his family, or the security of the city as a whole, said prisoner is held in a facility within Cat's Keep known as the Tower. This tall, narrow structure is situated just far enough from the keep wall to make a jump impossible even for the best athlete. The next closest building to the Tower is the vast central watch house. The Tower is four stories tall and is mostly stairs, with a single excellently appointed suite at the top, complete with physically fit servants that are able to run up and down the tall tower all day.

The Tower is guarded, but prisoners are primarily on their honor to behave as their status requires, and it is well known that several common spells for *levitation* and similar could easily free any Tower prisoner. Since Tower prisoners are never truly dangerous sorts, when they have escaped in the past, they often become the talk of Cat's Cradle for years, romantic folk heroes or villains, depending on their crimes. Most Tower prisoners are too concerned with appearances, dignity, and honor to escape, however. They more often hire teams of advocates to get them freed by legal means.

Adventure Hook: One of the prisoners in the Tower has important information to give, but for some reason (possibly a family or old business relationship) they divulge the information only to one of the characters, and the information turns out to be very valuable … and very dangerous to know.

C-10. The Watch House

Several old defensive structures from before the raising of Cat's Cradle's outer walls are built into the keep's inner wall. The largest of these — stretching from just beside the keep gate to cover nearly a third of its inner wall — has long since become the central headquarters, barracks, and short-term jail of the city watch. All watch captains for all districts, at least in theory, report here to Watch Commander **Reese Gavel**, with the sole exception of the Baronial Constabulary, whose leadership report directly to the baron.

Reese Gavel is an iron-haired half-elf of stiff posture and little imagination. She is good with a blade and better with organizational administration, taking a no-nonsense policy toward criminal behavior at all levels of society. She keeps a clean but spartan watch house and has done a serviceable job at maintaining order in all parts of Cat's Cradle, other than the Old City, where her every plan seems to fail, time and again, to her terse and stony frustration. She is also known to be on poor terms with Captain **Leesis Estromyl** of the Jade District Watch, but she is unable to dismiss him for reasons not openly discussed.

Adventure Hook: This is the jail. Breaking a prisoner out of jail is a classic adventure hook, and never, ever goes as planned.

Dockside District

The bustling waterfront is at the heart of Cat's Cradle, and though its importance has been somewhat eclipsed by the newer facilities in the Panhandle, Dockside remains a critical element of the city's economic and social life. Much of the current dock facility is less than a century old, dating back to the period in which all cargo, including alchemicals and supplies, was shipped through the main dock district, with some alchemical labs built there for convenience as well. With very little oversight, these labs grew in size and safety procedures became increasingly lax. Mishandling of alchemical runoff and an error in titration led to a massive explosion that raged through the docks, burning much of the district to the waterline. In the catastrophe's aftermath, the barony took direct control of the docks, began rebuilding, and declared that all alchemical products and supplies would be shipped through facilities in the Panhandle. Today, the rebuilt Dockside facilities are visited by a constant flow of lake vessels along with rowdy crews and the crime and vice that normally plagues the waterfronts of larger cities.

D-1. Baronial Constabulary

This ancient, four-story building serves as headquarters for the Baronial Constabulary, a branch of city law enforcement that is distinct from the city watch and other authorities. Overworked, understaffed, underpaid, and underfunded, the constabulary nonetheless exists as an independent entity devoted to investigating crimes that threaten the barony or the city as a whole. In practice, this means that the constabulary serves as a major crimes unit with the authority to look into offenses such as treason, smuggling, murder, arson, and similar illegalities. While theoretically superior to all other legal entities in the city, constabulary operatives frequently encounter resistance and pushback from members of the watch and private security groups, such as those hired to keep order in Old City. The constabulary is often viewed by these groups as a meddling, officious bunch of do-gooders with little regard for the realities of Cat's Cradle society. The animosity goes both ways, for many constables believe the watch to be corrupt or full of ineffectual time-servers. Though the constabulary operated with the full support of the baron, its members are usually on the verge of being overwhelmed by a tide of crime and graft.

Nevertheless, the constables carry on under the eccentric leadership of **Lady Genera,** a wizened and seemingly frail old woman whose unassuming appearance conceals a cunning mind and an unyielding, steely spirit. Lady Genera never raises her voice, is ceaselessly polite and deferential, and spends much of her time reading, sipping tea, and knitting or tatting, producing countless shawls and doilies which she gives as gifts to successful constables. Her dedication to the constabulary is unbreakable, however, and once she has undertaken an investigation, she stops at nothing to see it to its conclusion. Criminals who underestimate Lady Genera never make the same mistake twice. No one is entirely certain where she came from or how she got the job, but those who know her have no doubt about her dedication, intelligence, or ruthless efficiency.

Genera's second-in-command is the gruff Commander **Francovis Mageran,** a former watch officer who led an investigation into corruption and exposed a conspiracy to smuggle stolen alchemical salts out of Cat's Cradle. Resulting arrests and convictions resulted in watch officers turning against Mageran and branding him a traitor, but also earned him command of the constabulary. He remains a villain to most watch members, who still believe that he betrayed his colleagues, despite their provable wrongdoing. Mageran and Lady Genera's other senior investigators vet each new recruit to the constabulary, carefully researching their backgrounds and abilities to make certain that they will serve the barony loyally.

The constabulary is also a relatively small group of professional investigators, with 16 regular constables who carry silver badges in the shape of a snarling cat's head. They are commanded by five senior constables called investigators who bear gold badges. Uniforms are generally not worn while on duty, and even badges are not required, especially if constables are working undercover. All constables are authorized to enter any dwelling, seize any required evidence, and interrogate any appropriate individuals, and though they themselves cannot arrest suspects, constables are empowered to direct the watch to do so. The major exception to this rule is in the Old City, where the watch's conspicuous absence allows the constabulary to actually make arrests and file charges.

Members of the constabulary are a tough, uncompromising lot, well used to the grit and corruption of the city at large and always ready to defend their authority. Often expected to work alone, constables of all ranks are skilled fighters, often with roguish or magical skills as well. Specialist investigators provide magical, druidic, or divine assistance. Once a constable is on a case, only death or specific orders from superiors stops the investigation before it is complete.

Adventure Hook: The characters are deputized to serve as constables after several of the regular constables are removed from service (sick, killed, kidnapped, or whatever might be related to a sinister plot). The first order of business is to find out what has happened and why.

D-2. Veyloura Mercantile Enterprises

Managed by a partnership of two humans — **Barlund Halstead** and **Feona Indrik** — and the dwarf **Nurjal Hurgin,** Veyloura Mercantile Enterprises controls a fleet of five river-ships, countless barges, and finances regular caravans to and from the city. The partnership is known to be a troubled one, with coldly polite relations between its members even at the best of times. Conflicts over business plans and investments sometimes boil over into angry arguments, and in some cases, even blows have been exchanged. Nevertheless, the business continues to thrive and has made the tumultuous partners quite wealthy, leading them to stay together despite their struggles.

Unfortunately, the personality conflicts between three very assertive individuals cannot be papered over forever. Barlund, the oldest partner, has the most experience in business and has grown increasingly cautious over the years, averse to risks and focused primarily on protecting his existing investments and passing on a legacy of wealth to his three children. The business is named for Barlund's late sister, who died when he was a child. Nurjal is a brash, middle-aged dwarf from a wealthy and accomplished clan who turned his back on his family's assets, insisting that he could become rich on his own. He succeeded admirably in this task, but in the process developed an independent streak that has recently cause further estrangement from his human partners. Finally, Feona is the youngest and most daring of the trio, spending considerable funds on dead-end investments and wild schemes, some of which actually succeeded, further encouraging her incautious practices. Tensions between the three have escalated as each has gone their own way, placing relatives and cronies in important positions, further straining interpersonal relations.

The cold war power struggle to control Veyloura Enterprises may grow hot as Barlund and his children seek to contain the increasingly erratic behavior of Feona and her younger sister, and the thoughtless activities of Nurjal and his clansfolk, who have recently been acting independently and keeping excess profits from their specific enterprises for themselves, while Feona and Nurjal are developing their own plans to take sole control of Veyloura. When legitimate means fail, those close to the family believe that the entire situation may descend into all-out civil war, a situation which could engulf much of Dockside.

Adventure Hook: Other than the characters getting involved in the cold war among the partners of Veyloura Enterprises, the company is also a good source of any kind of adventure where characters are hired to rescue a mercantile operation. This could include fighting pirates, rescuing a stranded ship, guarding a caravan, etc.

D-3. Cat's Cradle Port Authority

As baronial income from the Panhandle docks is limited, most tariffs and taxes are levied on the main docks, where baronial assessors check each incoming vessel's cargo and assess fees, which must be collected before ships can offload. Chief Assessor **Elovan Avezila** leads a staff of assessors and their assistants who work in shifts around the clock. The port authority has a number of facilities, including a vault that contains collected income, which are transported to Cat's Keep in a well-guarded procession each week, and a small warehouse that houses confiscated contraband or cargo seized due to non-payment of fees. As might be expected, this warehouse is heavily guarded and a frequent target of burglary attempts. Though Avezila is considered to be an honest and hardworking individual, he has proved largely ineffectual in counteracting graft and bribery among his subordinates.

Fees and tariffs are assessed using a complex set of guidelines in which essential items such as basic foodstuffs, brickmaking supplies, and alchemical equipment are relatively lightly taxed, and items such as alcohol, textiles, livestock, artworks, and the like are assessed on a sliding scale. Fees are due immediately and most captains come prepared having already calculated and budgeted for them, but there are exceptions. Those who do not have sufficient

gold to pay their fees are subject to boarding and the impoundment of cargo equal to the value of the owed fees, and it is something of an open secret that confiscated cargos sometimes "mysteriously" disappear in the night, to be sold in Cat's Cradle by shady entrepreneurs or representatives of criminal families.

Adventure Hook: Though they represent an important aspect of Cat's Cradle's economic well-being, assessors are not incorruptible, and corruption tends to creep into the job despite the baron's continuing attempts to stamp it out. Though most assessors are honest men and women, some are open to bribery, usually accepting small handouts in exchange for looking the other way and going a little light on fees or tariffs. Such minor violations may lead to larger crimes as assessors are blackmailed or enticed with greater payoffs. In the end, some assessors have been culpable in outright smuggling, theft, and the sale of contraband from the port authority's warehouse. Find them.

D-4. The Sailor's Tavern

Run by bona fide old salt sailor **Tersa Skollet**, the Sailor's Tavern offers exactly what's on the package, providing those who crew lake vessels with accommodation, victuals, and entertainment. Those who suggest that river sailors are less boisterous and hard-living than their seagoing brethren are advised to spend some time at establishments like the Sailor's Tavern to see the error of their ways. Tersa's place is in constant tumult, with ships' crews and stevedores freely mixing, carousing, and fighting. In addition to fights (at least one is guaranteed each night), Tersa also offers gambling of all sorts, potables from the grittiest cheap ale to high-end elven liquors, food of all grades, and social or intimate companionship for those who can afford it. Accommodations are available as well, on the same type of sliding scale, with single hammocks going for 1 cp per night, on up to the tavern's luxury suite for 5 gp, with a variety of rooms in between.

The tavern's most popular pursuits are its somewhat extralegal ones, specifically the fighting pit that Tersa maintains in her sub-cellar. This cylindrical pit mimics the larger gladiatorial rings of big cities, with seating and standing room around its lip, high above the sandy floor. Here, combats take place between humanoid participants, wild animals, or single warriors against monstrous opponents. Drunken sailors bellow encouragement, ale is spilled, bets are laid, gold changes hands, brawls break out, and grudges are settled in the pit. Fights are rarely to the death, though this has been known to happen, especially when monsters are involved, and magic is forbidden, but otherwise Tersa's sub-cellar is probably the premiere private fight club in Cat's Cradle.

While theoretically the Sailor's Tavern is open to all, non-sailors are generally frowned upon and may find themselves ignored, insulted, or even challenged to a brawl in the fighting pit. Those who can hold their own against the aggressive regulars may earn themselves a place at the tavern, but so far few have bothered to even try, leaving Tersa's establishment to its familiar crowd.

D-5. The Gilded Barge

Though Cat's Cradle is a relatively small city, its waterfront is every bit as wild as those of larger settlements, and like most other port regions, Cat's Cradle boasts its share of brothels. The Gilded Barge is probably the city's best known such establishment, owned and operated by the gangsters of the Kennock Syndicate. Manager **Orloff Murgin** was recruited from a distant metropolis and was brought here to organize and oversee the business. Over the past five years, he has transformed the Barge into a successful moneymaker with a combination of mercantile acumen and ruthless suppression of the competition. Orloff is not a kind or merciful manager, but he is an efficient one, which keeps his employers happy.

Adventure Hook: Located in the rough-and-tumble docks, most would expect the Gilded Barge to cater mostly to sailors and waterfront workers, but Orloff's efforts have paid off in many ways, including by attracting a steady stream of nobles and wealthy clients from the Jade and Gold districts who venture here in groups, usually escorted by well-paid guards to keep trouble at bay. The characters might be hired as guards or hired to waylay one of these groups for various reasons.

D-6. Warehouse Number Six

One of a number of warehouses on the docks where cargo is stored before and after loading, this particular warehouse is owned by **Geldrin Thalkus**, one of the most successful of Cat's Cradle's merchants. It is cavernous and capable of holding cargo from several ships at once and is rented out to other merchants when space is available. Warehouse Number Six is therefore popular with smaller enterprises, more so because Thalkus is careful to keep the place secure and well-guarded.

Adventure Hook: Thalkus is a good patron for any kind of business-related adventure such as investigating thefts, recovering stolen goods, or stopping sabotage. In this case, if he hires the characters to investigate a theft from the warehouse, he will not want the theft to become common knowledge, since the place is supposed to be secure. The investigation will need to be delicate and completely secret.

D-7. The Doleful Wayfarer

This trim and brightly colored vessel serves as the floating headquarters for **Sargash Uthark** (see *Fortune Hunters*), an orcish mariner who spent years of carefully saved income from dozens of successful voyages and invested in a small fleet of ships for lake commerce. He currently owns controlling interest in five ships, all of which carry produce, sand, clay, and alchemical components into Cat's Cradle, and bear bricks, glassware, finished alchemicals, and other exports to other towns and cities in the region. His crews consist mostly of veterans that Sargash met during his days at sea, plus promising newcomers, and all are highly capable, braving the dangers of the lake as they efficiently sail from port to port.

The *Doleful Wanderer* is the pride of Sargash's fleet, a two-masted schooner crewed by 20 of his best sailors. Sargash runs his entire business out of his small cabin, where he maintains his books and records, leaving only minimal space for his own comfort. Despite its value as Sargash's headquarters, the *Wanderer* also plies the lake trade, though her limited cargo space makes speed and efficiency vital. Due to the hazards of lake travel, the vessel sports two ballistae that can be set up in a matter of minutes, and all of the crew are skilled fighters trained in techniques for dealing with the lake's more dangerous denizens. Sargash is reluctant to take the ship on especially hazardous missions, for its loss would be devastating to his business, and would place him and his most trusted crew in peril. For the most part, when not secure at the Cat's Cradle docks, the *Doleful Wanderer* sticks to safe, relatively easy coastal routes, well away from the deeper portions of the lake, making quick runs to and from various nearby ports.

D-8. Pierfront Fish Market

Though the yield of fish from nearby waters has declined recently due to the effects of alchemical runoff and pollution, fisherfolk are accustomed to sailing beyond this area and eagerly bring their supposedly untainted catch to Cat's Cradle for market day each week. On the market's off days, the booths and ground cloths of the market are still occupied by people selling dry goods, fruits and vegetables, utensils, and other gear, but the weekly market day draws throngs of folk from within the city and beyond. Lake fish of all sorts are available at the market — perch, trout, pickerel, even the occasional sturgeon — as well as crayfish, freshwater mussels, and other items.

A local species called the river tiger is a predatory fish like a large freshwater pike, but striped black and green — these constitute a rare catch but are considered a special delicacy and larger individuals draw considerable attention. Big lake tigers are much sought-after by trendy nobles and merchants, and some have been known to trigger bidding wars, with ownership of the fish considered a significant social coup.

Adventure Hook: Once bought, lake tigers are prepared by the finest chefs available and are served at exclusive gatherings, bringing significant notoriety to the hosts. Stories are told about nobles who compete for the ownership of a single river tiger to the point of espionage, brawls, and even duels, some of which spread to the fish market itself. The characters are hired to foil the success of a rival's banquet by sabotaging the fish course.

D-9. Hiring Hall

Sailing, dockwork, and fishing are seasonal positions, and turnover is high as business ebbs and flows. This old and outwardly dilapidated building is where captains, business owners, fishermen, sailors, barge tenders, stevedores, and others visit when hiring or looking for work. The hall is always crowded during the busy seasons of spring and summer, as there are plenty of fishing and lake transportation jobs. Employers occupy booths or desks inside the cavernous main hall, with signs or barkers to announce their pay rates and needs. Interviews with prospective hires are short and to the point, with contracts signed and advances paid on the spot. This is necessary in most cases, as vessels usually ship out as soon as they have full crews.

The hiring hall is sometimes the scene of chicanery as competing enterprises try to steal desirable crew from each other by loudly offering higher pay, interrupting interviews, and even stealing rivals' pay chests. As a result, guards are often employed to keep mayhem to a minimum, but even so, the hall is a place of shouting, noise, and crowds in the busy season. During the fall and winter, of course, hiring trails off, finally leaving the hall empty and echoing forlornly by midwinter.

Adventure Hook: The characters get caught up in a good old-fashioned brawl.

D-10. The Dockside Wall

These days, this battlemented wall serves more as a demarcation line between the Docks and Old City than any sort of defensive measure. Damage from the Dockside fire a century ago was never repaired, and most of the remainder has not been maintained over the decades, leaving some sections on the verge of collapse. Its wall walk is no longer safe and is not patrolled, nor with the exception of Eastwatch Tower, is it garrisoned in any way. The entire wall has degenerated from protection to threat over generations, and buildings in its shadow are extremely cheap to live in or purchase due to the imminent possibility of disaster. Enterprising locals have shored up the wall in some places in a variety of ways, some more effectively than others, but not a week goes by without at least one incident of a loose stone injuring or killing an incautious pedestrian or damaging one of the buildings below.

D-11. Eastview Tower

The only portion of the Dockside Wall that remains in semi-decent repair, Eastview Tower serves as headquarters for the Dockside city watch, housing 50 patrol members and their commander, Captain **Cyrus Alvi**, a rather morally ambiguous individual who values order over law and is willing to let petty crimes and corruption slide so long as overall peace and quiet is maintained. Despite the tower's central location between two major districts, Alvi's patrols focus almost exclusively on the Docks, leaving Old City to its own devices. Barracks occupy the bottom two levels of the tower, while Captain Alvi's quarters and the unit's extensive armory fill the third. The roof has been extensively rebuilt and reinforced and features a watch post and ballista, though the weapon is primarily there for show and to demonstrate that the watch is there.

Adventure Hook: Petty crooks (or at higher levels, the Thieves' Guild) hire the characters to "encourage" several of the patrol members to overlook a small crime. This is supposed to be just a payoff, but things go very wrong at the handoff of cash when a rival to the characters' employer either calls in the constabulary or tries to steal the money, leading to a potential scandal and also some missing money.

D-12. Sailors' Temple

Space is at a premium on the waterfront, so the various priesthoods who represent the lake sailors and fisherfolk have been forced to share space in this ornate structure, which is centrally located on the docks and open at all hours. The deity with the largest congregation is Kamien, goddess of rivers, lakes, springs and other bodies of fresh water. She is quite popular with the people who work on the lake, especially given that she provides protection from dangers such as storms, floods, and monsters. Priestess **Amnera Pasean** and her four acolytes see to the lake workers' spiritual needs, lead services, bless boats, provide healing and comfort, and even give aid and support to the jobless, bereaved, and the poor among the Docks' denizens. Some locals also revere Quell, who is normally a god of the sea but is believed by many to watch over all sailors and other folk who make their livings on the water. Quell's priest **Singlo Parzion** and his assistant provide their god's blessing to his worshippers, who often revere Kamien as well. A few other gods also maintain facilities at the temple, including Thyr, Freya, and Belon the Wise, though their priests work here part-time, giving the remainder of their attention to other temples elsewhere in the city.

Adventure Hook: This temple can be used for any religious quest sort of hook or as a good jumping off point for an assignment to fight pirates, always a good standby.

The Gold District (aka "Coin City")

The Gold District, commonly called "Coin City," is not as wealthy as the luxurious Jade region, but it is where the most money changes hands, as it is home to many shops, businesses, and mercantile enterprises, leading to its popular nickname. At its height, the district was a truly beautiful one, with white stone buildings and green slate roofs predominating. While Cat's Cradle's prosperity has continued since those days, the concentration of wealth among the city's upper classes has meant that some parts of Coin City have begun to fall into disrepair, and while the beautiful homes of the rich remain prominent, some neighborhoods are in decline, with poverty and want gaining an expanding toehold. Unlike the Old City, which has been largely left to its own devices by the city watch, the Gold District is still patrolled in most areas, and rampant crime is confined to its poorer sections such as the Warrens (**Location G-19**).

G-1. The Haunted Gate (aka Gold Gate)

This ornate archway is nearly 300 years old and features carvings of a number of unknown gods or heroes, and inscriptions in a variety of languages, some of which are so worn as to be illegible. Given its location, the gate naturally sees heavy traffic in and out of Alchemists' Alley and the wealthy enclaves of the Jade District. Nevertheless, the gate is treated with superstitious reverence by many of Cat's Cradle's folk, who believe it to be haunted or otherwise subject to supernatural phenomena.

There is some reason for this, as on certain nights, especially in the fall, some of the gate's inscriptions fluoresce with eerie pink light, and spectral figures have been sighted on walls near the gate, only to disappear when investigated. Other unconfirmed stories speak of whispered voices that can be heard by certain people while passing through the gate, or of strange dreams in which the Haunted Gate itself stands shimmering in strange landscapes.

Officially, the baron personally discourages these stories, suggesting that they are wild rumors or the figments of people's imaginations, but some believe otherwise. A few have taken it upon themselves to make independent arcane investigations of the gate, leading to a variety of theories, some more plausible than others. Some believe that ancient stones imbued with primal magic were used in the gate's construction and that the stones' latent energies produce strange but harmless effects. Others formulate more ominous theories, suggesting that the gate was once the site of demon worship and blood sacrifice and that it continues to leech the life energies of those who pass through it. Most alarmingly, some theorists believe that the gate itself is still active and once it gains enough power, it will show its true nature, opening up to some hellish or abyssal realm and unleashing terrors onto Cat's Cradle. This last suggestion is considered by most to be alarmist nonsense, though it has a small but dedicated circle of believers.

G-2. Calibos Inn

Ceil Carveth owns this inn, which is a popular destination for visitors to the Gold District. The building is quite old, dating from the founding of Cat's Cradle, when it was one of the first stone structures in the area. While renovating the old building a decade ago, Ceil found numerous artifacts from the old city, many of which he keeps on display at the inn's main dining hall. These include fragments of old statuary, clothing, banners, holy symbols, tools, and even weapons, all reflecting the structure's varied uses over the years, from a residence to a temple to the home of a mercenary adventuring band. The inn's name comes from the leader of this group of adventurers who perished 22 years ago at the hands of an angry demon.

Most of Ceil's collection are items of historical interest but of little real value, but there are a few exceptions that he keeps safely locked away and shows only to select visitors. These include a fine sword that somehow survived the passing years untouched by rust or corrosion and a similarly untouched round shield emblazoned with a northern-style black dragon on a red enameled field. Ceil suspects that the items are magical and of deep historical importance, but for reasons he cannot quite fully explain, he has chosen not to investigate their provenance or to have them properly identified, preferring instead to keep them safe in a locked chest in his quarters. His desire to protect the items has grown greater, to the point that he has had a poison needle trap installed on the chest to ward off would-be thieves.

Aside from his growing obsession with these two treasures, Ceil and his brother **Danelos** run a tidy and pleasant inn, serving good food at good prices and providing overviews of the city, its history, and its culture to those who might be visiting from distant lands. Rooms are available at standard rates and are comfortable but not excessively luxurious, further enhancing the Calibos Inn's reputation as a pleasant and economical destination.

Adventure Hook: Collectors like Ceil are always good for a "find it and bring it to me" sort of adventure; in this case, it's probably something once owned by the adventurer Calibos, a shoe or perhaps his helmet. Alternatively, one of the items in Ceil's collection may have gone missing and require the characters to track it down.

G-3. The Baronial Arts Ministry

This sturdy, utilitarian, and somewhat bland-looking three-story structure houses the offices of the Baronial Arts Ministry, a small group of nobles and civil officials who oversee performances and events at the plaza and elsewhere. The uppermost floor contains miscellaneous items needed for performances and presentations, as well as props, banners, instruments, and other items from previous events. These are kept here and taken out as needed. The second floor houses the offices of the ministry. **Lord Minister Norris Prebble** painstakingly oversees the organization, carefully scheduling and monitoring events in a manner that generally drives their participants to madness. Rumor has it that Lord Prebble, husband of the wealthy and politically powerful **Lady Marta Prebble**, was given this assignment by a frustrated Baron Scale who tired of Norris' constant presence and meddling in affairs of state.

The ground floor contains offices and ready rooms and is generally used by the staff who prepare and present the various events. A small watch post is located on the ground floor and is home to six watch members who patrol the area.

Adventure Hook: Prevent a riot or other disturbance at one of the plaza performances (see **Location G-4**). This might be something planned by a radical political element.

G-4. The Baronial Plaza

Six columns of fine, imported, white-veined pink marble flank the smooth and near-seamless paving stones of the Baronial Plaza. Constructed 60 years ago by one of Baron Scale's predecessors, the plaza stands at the heart of the Gold District and is a gathering-place for all the folk of Cat's Cradle. It is used for a wide range of activities, from addresses by the baron himself, to open-air markets, processions, festivals, concerts, and plays. The plaza ends in a white marble arch that encloses a curved acoustical shell that allows even the most distant listener to hear words spoken on the raised stage.

G-5. Salt Ale Corner

Stephan Kadhrossa owns this prime piece of property located conveniently near the colorful events of the Baronial Plaza, from which he sells ales and beers from local brewers. Kadhrossa sells by the barrel to taverns, and during plaza events to the general public by the mug. Regular customers even bring their own drinking vessels so that they can fill up at Salt Ale Corner and carry their potables to the nearby event. Kadhrossa's wares are far superior to the watered-down drinks served by plaza vendors.

The establishment's name comes from Kadhrossa's signature salt ale, which is brewed at his estate outside Cat's Cradle, where certain alchemical salts are incorporated into the process. The exact salts and their proportions are understandably a closely guarded secret, and all Kadhrossa says is that if anyone ever tried to copy it, and their formulae were off even by a fraction, it would result in widespread sickness and even death. This of course begs the question of how the formula was discovered in the first place, but Kadhrossa, his family, and employees maintain a wall of silence regarding the topic.

Adventure Hook: A secret meeting is to be held here between two river-captain pirates. The characters might be hired to protect one or both of the captains or to capture one or both of them. The patron for this adventure might be law enforcement or it might be a third-party rival to both captains.

G-6. The Celestial Theater

Officially owned and operated by the barony, the Celestial is a grand theater open to all, and scene of plays, concerts, operas, and many other varied performances. A round stage in the center of the main auditorium is viewable by the audience from all angles. The stage is surrounded by the standing-room only area known popularly as "The Pit," which is invariably crowded with boisterous patrons who paid 1 cp or less to attend and who have few qualms about drinking, brawling, or shouting encouragement to those on the stage. Above the Pit are the plain benches of the Gallery, where most ordinary Cat's Cradlers sit — while they too can freely eat and drink, their reactions to events on stage are usually less vehement than those from the Pit. Above the Gallery are the Luxury seats: roomy, padded, and tended by obsequious theater staff.

The most exclusive seats in the theater are the private boxes, which are usually reserved for nobles or especially generous "friends" of the theater. Prices vary greatly, with some performances demanding unbelievably high rates — up to 500 gp per person for a private box during an especially popular or in-demand performance. Other prices are less outrageous — luxury seats range from 1–10 gp, while the gallery costs 1 sp, and the Pit is usually 1 cp, though in some cases attendance in the Pit is entirely free. Food and drink are available with quality and prices commensurate with their seating area.

Stage manager **Chaffin Kyle** is a veteran actor whose long and storied career was highlighted by some of the most ferociously bad reviews in kingdom history, and whose vainglorious personality continues to attract comment. Despite his bombastic and overwhelming conduct, Kyle is nonetheless a decent manager who efficiently oversees productions and has managed to obtain the services of a number of talented performers. Recently, the grand opera *Macobert the Conqueror* opened to rave reviews, with packed houses each night, attended twice by Baron Scale and his family.

Though the opera continues to be a smash hit, rumors have begun to circulate that the opera company has somehow been cursed, as minor accidents have plagued the show, and in several cases, important crew members have been injured. When lead singer **Abrosus Wegnor** — a famous tenor who is said to have risen to prominence from the teeming slums of Castorhage — fell ill and was unable to sing, his part went to understudy **Bram Philomath**, a relative newcomer who nonetheless received glowing reviews for his performance. Once he had recovered his voice, Abrosus demanded to be put back in the lead role, but he was tragically killed in a fall from the risers. Though none of this could be directly attributed to any outside cause, material or supernatural, the tragedy stoked the rumors even further and, coincidentally, kept the houses full every night, with wealthy attendees going to far as to sit in the Gallery or, in a few cases, the Pit, in the hopes of witnessing drama both on and off stage.

Adventure Hook: Bram has a secret: A guardian spirit is trying to protect him despite his own wishes, and it is this spirit that is responsible for the problems. The nature of the spirit could be anything from an imp to a demon, depending on the level of the characters.

G-7. Eastriver Wall

Dividing the western parts of Cat's Cradle from the verdant but hazardous strip of Alchemists' Alley, Eastriver Wall is constantly kept in good repair, regularly patrolled and, with its opposite number on the other side of the Quicksilver River, serves as something of an icon, symbolizing Cat's Cradle's strength and prosperity. Originally a grim gray stone fortification, the wall has been faced with white granite like many of the homes in the Gold District, and its towers house well-equipped squads of city watch who regularly patrol the less poor sections of Coin City. The walls facing Alchemists' Alley have been extensively reinforced to guard against the dangers of fires or explosions.

G-8. Pearl Apartments

Typical of high-rent rooming houses in Coin City, the Pearl boasts everything from single-room apartments to multi-room suites on the upper floors, all at premium rates. Smaller accommodations cost about 100 gp per month, while luxury suites may cost 10 times as much. Apartments at the Pearl are almost always available due to their high cost, but the management, a consortium of local nobles and entrepreneurs led by senior partner **Khelias Eversol**, insists that tenants pass a careful background check to weed out frauds or troublemakers. Adventurers are especially discouraged from staying here, as the owners are unapologetic in their dislike for what Khelias herself refers to as "wastrels" and "hobos."

Khelias, her associates, and manager **Sir Anteo Macarvid** — a retired knight given the position largely due to the prestige his name attracts — are determined to maintain the Pearl's reputation whatever the cost, but their efforts were severely complicated when **Osuras Kelmar**, the wealthy inhabitant of the Pearl's top floor, was stabbed to death in a brutal and thus far unsolved murder. Wary of publicity, Khelias and Anteo have avoided conventional procedures, asking their friends in the watch to quietly look into the matter, though few have real experience in detailed criminal investigation skills. So far, they have kept the crime secret from the constabulary, who at this point are the most appropriate investigators, but whose no-nonsense procedures might disrupt the Pearl's daily life or bring unwanted attention from the public. Should the constables discover that they have been left out of the loop, however, they are certain to respond aggressively.

Adventure Hook: The situation has grown even more untenable with a second murder, that of a young up-and-coming alchemist named **Milo Bren**, who like Osuras Kelmar was stabbed to death in his own apartment, and almost no evidence — physical, arcane, or otherwise — was left behind. Desperate, Khelias has turned for help to a group that she despises — freelance adventurers — to help her solve the mystery and catch the culprit before the constabulary catches wind of the incident and shuts her precious Pearl down for the investigation.

G-9. Scolren's Gate

Named for the baron who extensively renovated and strengthened the gate years ago, this portal is crafted of pink granite and carved with the faces and names of various old gods and heroes.

G-10. The Greens

This neighborhood is named for the large number of old, decaying green slate roofs that remain here, a legacy of its past wealth and influence. The Greens is typical of the poor and rundown sections of the otherwise prosperous Coin District and is a place of narrow streets — many bereft of paving stones and left to decay into mucky, rutted pathways — badly repaired and patched walls, fallen roofs, and tottering lost grandeur. The Greens contains homes mostly for laborers who work elsewhere in the district, as well as a few disreputable taverns and gambling houses. Assault, robbery, and other crimes of violence are common here, where the watch patrols only sporadically. Those watch members who do deign to come here are susceptible to bribery and all too happy to look the other way if it saves them from the excessive labor of arrest and actual law enforcement.

Adventure Hook: A small group of street vendors and merchants from the neighborhood approach the characters and offer to pay them if they can bring order to the area.

G-11. College Dormitory

In contrast to luxury residences like the Pearl, this featureless brick three-story structure contains accommodations for students at the Alchemists College (**Location J-1**). Rooms are spare, shared by two students, and include a pair of cots or bunks, small chests for belongings, miniscule desks, and bookshelves, with two common baths and toilet facilities shared by all occupants of each floor.

The Dormitory (it has no real official name) is a wild and tumultuous place, as many students are boisterous and outspoken, given to excessive consumption of alcohol and other youthful folly, including frequent bed-hopping and sampling of questionable alchemical concoctions. The occasional spectacular fire or poisoning is dealt with by the squad of college trustees who occupy the main floor and deal with major incidents, though for the most part they turn a blind eye to minor infractions and youthful exuberance.

G-12. Academy Sales

The Achemical College in Jade District trains numerous students in the basic procedures of alchemy and allied crafts. Throughout the learning process, students create their own alchemicals, and those that serve a useful consumer purpose are sold at this old building, where they can be obtained at bargain rates. The faculty of the school naturally tests all items for potency and potential hazard, and of course does not sell anything that could be dangerous, limiting themselves to various low-level potions, cleaning supplies, crafting compounds, and generally useful products. Students and instructors work the establishment, maintaining stocks, performing inventory, and selling products, the proceeds of which are split between the academy and the students who made them. Thus, students make a bit of extra income, while the academy draws a steady income.

While most of the items sold here are, as noted, relatively minor goods with limited use, college representatives may make arrangements to sell more advanced or powerful alchemicals that have been crafted by advanced students. In such cases, potential buyers must directly contact the Alchemists' Guild and the college staff with specific needs to determine whether such products can be safely created and to verify the buyer's intentions and reputation. In such cases, the purchase takes place at Academy Sales under the watchful eye of college instructors.

Adventure Hook: A quantity of explosive stone essence that could be disguised as ordinary rocks or carved stone objects was recently delivered to Academy Sales for a supposedly respectable buyer, only to be stolen en route in a well-planned and well-executed operation. After this, the buyer mysteriously vanished and further investigation by the constabulary revealed that his identity, as a distinguished mage from a large city in the kingdom, was entirely falsified. The embarrassment to the college was matched only by the alarm of baronial authorities, who realized how dangerous the stolen substance could be. The overworked constabulary added the theft to its ever-growing list of open investigations and continues to pursue leads without success.

G-13. The Arcanum

The wizardly partners **Azoggo Afriedus** and **Salvatore of the Flame** operate this extensive and prestigious magic shop where they sell material components, wands, rings, potions, and other items to wealthy patrons and adventurers with gold burning holes in their pockets. However, Azoggo and Salvatore carefully avoid selling anything that might compete with the city's alchemists — potions fall into a gray area, but most are willing to leave those out of the discussion — as they want to avoid any business conflicts that might interfere with their income.

The shop is something of a wonder, its shelves packed with magic items of all kinds. Magical lighting and effects help direct customers to the items they seek, while imps and unseen servants aid the owners in obtaining goods and in collecting payments. As a rule, the partners offer what could be called "consumer-grade" magical items, usually of the more common variety, enhanced with low-level spells or providing only lesser effects. More prestigious or wealthy clients can talk to the pair about items of greater power, or even commission magical devices. Of course, such items are not kept on display but rather in illustrated catalogs available at the shop.

Adventure Hook: In addition to commissions and custom work, Azoggo and Salvatore do a thriving business with adventurers, sending them off to obtain saleable items, some of which are quite powerful and dangerous in the wrong hands. Naturally, they deal only with the most honest and well-established adventuring groups, for they know how easy it would be for their hired help to simply keep the items or sell them to the highest bidder. Should anyone contemplate cheating the partners, they find themselves ruthlessly hunted down, as Azoggo and Salvatore also have many contacts among the communities of bounty hunters, assassins, and spies.

G-14. Voles Gate

This gate is quite old and weathered, though thanks to its original design and builders, it remains quite sturdy and unbowed despite centuries of weather and traffic. Voles Gate forms the northern entrance to Cat's Cradle and is consequently busy at all hours, with throngs of travelers, farmers, merchants, and alchemists, on foot or mounted, alone or with caravans of carts and wagons. The gate is guarded, and goods entering and leaving are subject to inspection, though the sheer volume of traffic makes most inspections cursory at best. The gate is named for Voles, the next town on the caravan route in this direction.

G-15. Swallowtail Manor

While they are nouveau riche and haven't earned their place in Cat's Cradle's highest levels of society, **Asea Rohlind** and **Gellor Trendar** (see **Location B-9**) are the proprietors of the trendy and expensive up-and-coming Mystic Stone brickworks. Swallowtail Manor was a faded glory of the neighborhood, long neglected and fallen into disrepair when Gellor and Asea purchased it six years ago. They have since restored the place to a semblance of its former glory, though some neighbors have taken issue with their design choices and consider the new Swallowtail Manor to be a tribute to garish excess rather than the subtle beauties of the past. Swallowtail Manor boasts small but well-tended grounds with magical lighting and topiary enhanced by gnomish illusionists.

Originally, the manor was a prime example of local architecture with a main house crafted from sturdy stone and faced with white granite, and roofed with the green slate typical of the neighborhood. Since their arrival, Asea and Gellor have kept the home's clean white facing, but have replaced the battered slate tiles with their own brickwork, incorporating magical fluorescence that illuminates the area at night with a pale blue glow. Complaints from neighbors have been uniformly ignored, or complainers have been bought off with gifts and invitations to Asea and Gellor's lavish parties.

Adventure Hook: See **Locations B-7** and **B-9**.

G-16. Temple of Sefagreth

The great god of commerce is quite popular in Coin City, where would-be merchant princes seek their fortunes and businesses seek new customers and increased wealth. High Priest **Father Kel Aderock** is himself a successful merchant and importer who makes his permanent home in the Jade District, but spends much of his time pressing the flesh and making friends with the people of the local area. His sermons proclaiming the sanctity of wealth and (somewhat less vehemently) the need for charity are legendary, as are his "grand services" at the lavish temple which are little more than well-disguised parties for wealthy donors. As cities' founders' days are particularly sacred to Sefagreth's followers, Kel's services and celebrations on Cat's Cradle's traditional founding day are particularly lavish and well-attended.

Father Kel revels in his popularity and spends lavishly on the temple, his home, and himself, often making little distinction between his own income and temple funds. His natural charisma has also attracted considerable attention from the women in his congregation, who fill the front pews during his sermons, hanging on his every word. His romantic escapades with his more adoring followers are considered a bit unethical by church officials, but there are no specific rules against it, so Kel has become quite the ladies' man. Such is Kel's ego that he has begun to think of himself as irresistible and now he puts very little effort into keeping his amorous adventures secret, leaving a trail of broken hearts and angry partners in his wake.

The eventual outcome of Kel's activities remains to be seen, but it is also known that his superiors have begun to notice his misuse of church funds and are contemplating sending an inspector or senior cleric to provide oversight and, if necessary, official discipline. Such an event would be quite devastating to Kel and the church in general, so it will probably be done with great discretion and could end in the spendthrift Father Kel being transferred to a far less prestigious temple, perhaps on a distant and windswept island for a few years. This is assuming, of course, that a jilted lover or an angry spouse does not get to him first.

Adventure Hook: Sefagreth is a neutrally aligned god of trade, so any commerce-based adventure hook could begin here. As an example, the merchant Torgos Paite has had three of his last caravans attacked by a thief wearing a green scarf wrapped over his face. In each case, only a small amount of money was taken before the thief escaped, but Torgos wants the thief apprehended.

G-17. Quicksilver House

Senior alchemist **Osenshahle Warne** maintains a home here, though she increasingly spends her time at her lab in Alchemists' Alley. When she is at her lavish estate, she spends more and more time in study and research, even going so far as to engage in alchemical experimentation in the main house, an activity strictly forbidden by baronial edict. Warne's continued obsession with her experiments has led her to neglect her health and hygiene.

Exactly what Warne is looking for isn't known, even to her most intimate friends (of which she seems to have fewer and fewer), and of late she has grown even more secretive and hostile toward anyone who questions her. Of the handful of acquaintances and fellow alchemists with whom Warne still talks, several have expressed increasing concern for her life and sanity. They speculate that her research has taken her into unexplored territory, such as the search for immortality, the secrets of alchemically transmuting base metals to gold, the permanent artificial enhancement of her consciousness, or other obscure research, and that her obsession is affecting her mental health. Some even go so far as to suggest that Warne is using drugs or arcane means to allow her to work without rest, and that this is the source of her strange behavior.

Regardless, the once-magnificent Quicksilver House has grown chaotic and filthy, with piles of books, boxes of reagents, endless platters of uneaten food, and other detritus blocking doorways and jamming halls, filling some chambers from floor to ceiling. Warne keeps her workspace relatively clear, but even this area is cluttered and almost unlivable. Most of her servants have quit and those that remain despair of ever making any headway against the growing mountains of filth and clutter. Rats and other vermin have begun to spread from the estate and into neighboring structures, leading to calls for the barony to intervene and do something to help Warne, or at least to stem the tide somewhat. So far, these calls have gone unheeded, and Quicksilver house has continued to deteriorate.

Adventure Hook: Warne has indeed discovered something important, an alchemical formula that assists in opening planar gates. The problem is that one has opened on the premises, and dream-creatures are bleeding in through it.

G-18. Avar's Alchemicals

Avar Sul is not an alchemist, but he is a skilled broker and salesman who maintains the Gold District's most prestigious retail alchemical business in this three-story building. Sul caters to clients from across Cat's Cradle, even those from the more prestigious sections of the Jade District, as his product carries a significant cachet among the wealthy and influential. His main floor consists of sales space for inexpensive and benign alchemical supplies and products such as bismuth, sulfur, calamine, gypsum, charcoal, glass, and various harmless salts, as well as minor potions, salves, and tinctures. The second floor is home to more valuable substances such as silver, gems, gold, rare oils, and resins, and hazardous substances such as fulminates, arsenic, aqua fortis, caustic sodas, vitriols, corrosive sublimates, and the like. Valuable items are kept in locked chests behind cages or bars, while explosive, poisonous or corrosive items are carefully handled by Sul's well-qualified staff. Most of his employees are gnomes from well-known families with a reputation for alchemical and potion-making skills, and have a well-developed sense of caution and safety.

Avar's third floor is the most secure and important aspect of his business, as it contains items of extreme value or hazard, including many completed alchemical substances, ultra-rare reagents and reactants, valuable gems, and items of magical, extradimensional, or extremely hazardous natures. Only the most trusted of Avar's employees are allowed on this floor, and it is constantly guarded by a pair of alchemically enhanced iron golems who deal mercilessly with unauthorized visitors. Cognizant of past disasters, Avar is careful to keep the third floor totally secure and safe and is scrupulous in obeying baronial law, which decrees that no alchemical experimentation or manufacture can occur outside the Baronial Corridor. Every single item in the building is logged and carefully measured, with all changes noted and confirmed. Avar's collection of logbooks has grown so extensive that many are now stored in a warehouse in the Panhandle.

Adventure Hook: As Avar's reputation is of vital importance to him and his business, he is quick to deal with any irregularities. Recently, a number of important reagents turned up missing, and Avar's investigation revealed that his precious logbooks have been falsified. He has discreetly contacted the constabulary, noting that the culprit or culprits do not yet know that their deception has been revealed, and that a quiet investigation is called for. So far, Commander Mageran has cooperated, assigning senior operatives to the case and telling them to keep a very low profile. Senior Investigator **Mattea Theasean** (See *Fortune Hunters*), a veteran, highly capable detective, is currently in charge of the investigation and has begun to have dark suspicions. Though on the surface the incident seems like nothing more than employee pilferage, Theasean believes the importance of the stolen substances and the secrecy surrounding the crime suggest a deeper and far more troubling conspiracy at work. The characters are brought in through Mattea or are hired by the actual conspirators to impede the investigation.

G-19. The Warrens

The Warrens is a neighborhood of the Gold District completely unlike the rest of the area, for it is as deep a slum as the Old City. The Warrens are roughly bounded by Crosswise Road to the north, the Dockside wall to the south, and Scamper's Run to the east, although the delineation between the Warrens and Old City across Scamper's Run is more of a boundary between gang territories than quality of the neighborhoods, for the Gold District's ordinary flavor is much declined here. The shops of Scamper's Run are controlled by a gang called the Scampers, a violent crew that extorts money from the shopkeepers and vendors of the street. The Scampers do not venture into the Warrens themselves, which are loosely controlled by a gang called the Warreners. The Warreners are more tightly affiliated with the Thieves' Guild (see **Location O-17**) and with Old Kennock, although they are one of the independent organizations that make up the informal, outer parts of the Thieves' Guild.

Adventure Hook: The characters are recruited to assist either the Scampers or the Warreners in a battle for control of the other gang's territory.

THE JADE DISTRICT

The most recently completed section of the city, the Jade District first came into being as the Cat's Cradle's wealthiest began to flee the crumbling Old City just over a century ago. A large vein of a jade-colored marble-like stone was discovered near the Salchamp at around the same time, so much of the new wealthy district was constructed from this beautiful new stone (after consulting local alchemists and masons very thoroughly first).

Grand and imposing, with wide, clean streets and pompously lovely architecture, the Jade District is Cat's Cradle's wealthiest area, and everyone who is anyone lives there, with the notable exception of Baron Scale and his family, as described in the Cat's Keep section.

In addition to excessively large and fancy homes, the Jade District contains several elite guild houses, a few schools for the wealthy, surprisingly few taverns and public houses (though one expensive inn), and the sorts of shops and craftspeople that cater to a loftier clientele than those in the Gold District to the east.

J–1. THE ALCHEMISTS COLLEGE

In the northeastern quarter of the Jade District, along the Baronial Corridor wall, stands a newer jade-marble structure, recently built relative to the surrounding buildings. This is a local college for alchemists, conceived in an attempt to increase local respect among the elite for the often smelly and even explosive field of alchemy.

Despite the brooding grandeur of the college's exterior, its acceptance as an elite institution has not yet fully occurred. Most of the teachers and students do not hail from wealthy backgrounds, and those who do are in some cases in disgrace with their families. Nevertheless, lectures are crowded, and the school seems well-funded, if mostly by nouveau riche investors.

Within the main college edifice, all classes are book- and lecture-based, with little practical learning, as alchemical mixing is forbidden outside designated areas of the city. The college grounds, however, boast a private door into Alchemists' Alley, where more practical learning takes place.

Adventure Hook: Students at the college have a long tradition of very minor practical jokes using their skills, but these have recently taken a dark twist, becoming more dangerous. The faculty tends to ignore this, but the president of the college, Maurmab Doane, believes that an external force is influencing the students, possibly even controlling some of them.

J–2. ALL YOUR PROMISES

One of several shops along the Market of Promises to play its name off the market itself, All Your Promises is the storefront of locally celebrated jeweler Celesa Tolban. Known for her particular skill with gem-cutting and intricate silver working, Tolban has even received commissions for her work from nobles in the distant capital.

The jewelry available at All Your Promises is crafted by Tolban's army of apprentices, with Tolban herself working these days only on the highest-paying commissions or on art pieces of her own design. However, even the apprentices' baubles are never on display for the common rabble to wander in and view. Rather, the interior of All Your Promises' showroom features plush chaises, marble-topped tea-tables, fine art on the walls, and a few potted plants.

Customers who look as if they can afford fine jewels are offered refreshments and permitted to gaze upon the merchandise one velvet tray at a time. Anyone who does not look sufficiently moneyed is likely to be asked to leave by Drevon, a well-dressed, well-spoken, well-mannered, and exceedingly well-muscled half-orc who serves as the shop's primary greeter.

Adventure Hook: A unique stone given to the store for setting into a necklace has apparently been stolen, and Celesa needs to get it back or tell the customer of the theft. The last person who was near the bauble was a nondescript individual with a streak of white in his hair who was carrying a cage in which something appeared to be slithering around.

J–3. THE BARONIAL MANSION

Northwest of Pike Square and northeast of the Temple of Prosperity stands a gorgeous jade-marble structure known as the Baronial Mansion. When the elite of Cat's Cradle began fleeing the Old City for the Jade District, Scolren (great-grandfather to Baron Scale), the baron of the day, decided that Cat's Keep was insufficiently stylish for his tastes and began construction on this mansion. It is similar in size to the old keep, but more elegantly laid-out, and far less drafty. It is also, unlike Cat's Keep, constructed of the finest and most expensive materials available.

Second only to the Temple of Prosperity as one of Cat's Cradle's most ostentatious buildings, the baronial mansion is currently used only to house aristocratic visitors to the city, as Baron Scale has returned his family to the old keep. The baronial mansion's interior is filled with grandiose art from all over the world, much of it gifts the baronial family has received from other aristocrats and elites over time, and the rest commissioned by Baron Scolren or by Scale's grandmother, Baroness Escaulla. Only the portrait of the tragically short-tenured Baron Escallel, Scale's father, was commissioned more recently.

Because of the need to safeguard so many fine art pieces, the baronial mansion remains fully staffed at all times, including by a number of armed guards. **Mistress Fulchen Lakefell**, the captain of these guards as well as the head servant, went to school with Baron Scale's beloved father at Coldwater.

Adventure Hook: One of the pieces of fine art is a mimic that releases spores causing other art pieces to turn slowly into mimics. The mimic-spores might or might not have been introduced into the building deliberately.

J–4. THE BRANLITH CONSERVATORY

This prestigious music school occupies the single largest building on Jade Square and is known for several things. First and foremost, the best music teachers that can be enticed to Cat's Cradle are paid impressive salaries to offer their talents and wisdom to the conservatory's students, with often quite pleasing results. Second, while particular musical geniuses might receive scholarships to master their instruments here, the school's unspoken primary purpose has, over the years, become a place where the wealthy send young children to learn a bit of music and stage decorum before they are old enough to attend Coldwater Finishing School (**Location J-5**).

Third, the Branlith Conservatory serves as a concert venue for students and teachers at the conservatory, and for wealthy patrons to host concerts outside their own homes. For this reason, it is quite common for members of the public to be found wandering the school halls, often lost, as the conservatory's layout is complex and anything but intuitive.

Finally, in the construction of his conservatory, old Baronet Branlith (long deceased) had many of the walls enchanted to allow no sound to pass through them. His intention, probably innocent by all accounts, was to make certain that music students could practice confidently, even while still sounding terrible, and also to make certain that concerts would never be disturbed by loud sounds from outside, and could run late into the night without disrupting students' or neighborhood residents' sleep.

It has been noted, however, that the enchantments on the conservatory walls stop shouts, screams, and cries for help just as readily as strains of music. While no great scandal has ever yet touched the halls of the Branlith Conservatory, many believe that this is only a matter of time. Or perhaps the scandals have happened, but have all been covered up.

Adventure Hook: Forneo Ganuune, a famous poet from a distant city, is being held here for ransom by a group of lesser nobles who are down on their luck and saw the opportunity to raise some money with a bit of kidnapping.

Cat's Cradle
JADE DISTRICT
N
W
E
S
MAP J
POUCH OF COINS
ODDWATER WAY
CAT'S LEG
GUILD STREET
CROSSWIRE ROAD
SPITMONEY STREET
GREENSTONES
JADE SQUARE
MARKET OF PROMISES
1
2
3
4
5
6
7
8
9
10
11
12
13
14
15
16
17
18
19
20
21

J–5. Coldwater Finishing School

This stoic, gray structure near the southern edge of the Jade District is believed to be the district's oldest construction, long predating Cat's Cradle's western outer walls. The oldest parts of the building were once a rival fortress built by a disgruntled branch of the baronial family in a failed attempt to found a competing town across the Quicksilver. The two family branches reconciled generations ago, and the redundant fort came to be used as a fencing school for wealthy children instead.

Since then, the structure has been built up over time to its current size and granted by the baron to the illustrious Coldwater family. Though the Coldwaters are not, themselves, aristocrats, they are known to train fine personal servants and military officers and to provide schooling sufficient for even nobility. All the wealthiest families in Cat's Cradle send their adolescent children to the Coldwater Finishing School to learn etiquette, fencing, riding, ballroom dancing, and other elegant pursuits. The baron himself was schooled at Coldwater, though it is rumored that he does not plan to send his own children there. As the baron's children are currently too young to attend, this is, as yet, no more than a rumor.

Adventure Hook: Harsinn Coldwater, the head of school, received a note one of his teachers intercepted as it was being passed between two students. Upon reading it, he realized that one of the children overheard certain details about a plot to assassinate Lady Genera, the head of the Baronial Constabulary (see **Location D-1**).

J–6. Drello's Fine Garments

Everyone who is anyone in Cat's Cradle wears Drello's designs (or those of his apprentices). Drello has a storefront off the Market of Promises, and the younger apprentices tailor anything purchased there to fit a customer (if possible). However, far more prestige is reserved for those who wait for an appointment to meet with Drello face to face to have something personally designed on commission.

It can take up to six months to get a meeting with Drello, and up to three even to meet with his most advanced apprentices, so wearing a Drello creation to a local event takes considerable planning, even on top of the wild expense of his garments. That said, Drello does know how to make people look good in clothes, with a fine eye for how fabric hangs on any figure and what colors look best with what complexions (not just for human tones!). He is said to enjoy a challenge and dresses anyone who can pay.

J–7. Fethen Bank and Investment

A glowering gray structure off Pike's Square, Fethen Bank and Investment offers two services. First, the Fethen Vault is considered to be the safest and most magically impregnable storage facility in the region. The Fethen family has a stellar reputation for honesty and organization, and are easily wealthy enough to hire the best guards and wizards to protect their interests (and those of their clients). Renting space in the Fethen Vault is expensive, but considered to be well worth the price.

The Fethen family's other business, besides meticulous guarding and maintenance of their vault, is in investing. If Matriarch Fethen or her husband, or one of their four children, believes that a shipping venture, business, or other endeavor is likely to turn a profit, they loan or even grant money to said enterprise. They do not charge interest on their loans, but rather make their money back by contracting for percentages of an enterprise's profits.

All six of the family's decision-makers are shrewd and clever, unlikely to be tricked or to lend to a profitless venture, but their reputation is also for honesty, and for working with their clients to make certain that everyone makes money, not just the Fethens. That said, they are rarely interested in financing the enterprises of the poor or in giving money to people who really need it. The Fethens may be honest and may treat their clients well, but they are not precisely "nice."

Adventure Hook: The Fethens are useful for any commercial-type adventure. Most recently, two ships they invested in were sunk by a monstrous river-fish. One of the younger Fethens has become obsessed with the idea that the river-fish is somehow being deliberately sent to attack ships in which the Fethen family has an interest. The others disagree but are willing to hire adventurers to at least look into it.

J–8. Horizon's Promise

This elite (and elitist) art gallery is one of the more recently opened shops along the Market of Promises, but it has already become quite a wealthy establishment under the management of its part-owner **Fazalia Fane**. Horizon's Promise shows art and sculpture imported from all over the world, as well as from the kingdom's distant capital city (and notably very little from local artists). These pieces are sold at private auctions after their brief showing periods, for purportedly astronomical prices.

After a recent break-in and attempted theft of a risqué marble deity of love, security at Horizon's Promise has tightened considerably, and even entry to the gallery showroom is now permissible by invitation only. It is said that the Kennock Syndicate would give a tidy sum for such an invitation.

Adventure Hook: A series of six statues are scheduled to arrive at Dockside in two days, and Fazalia received an anonymous tip from someone that the statues are to be stolen by the Kennock Syndicate on their way to the gallery. Naturally, she is concerned, partly because the existence of the statues was believed to be secret in the first place.

J–9. The Jade District Watch House

The Jade District Watch House, just down the street from the Market of Promises, is one of the larger gray buildings in the southern Jade District. Originally constructed before the Jade District existed, this fortress-like facility was intended to be the watch house for the entire west side of Cat's Cradle, early in the town's expansion across the river. After the exodus of the wealthy from the Old City, however, and the springing up of the Jade District, this watch house was ultimately assigned to the Jade District only and later even walled off from the Panhandle District.

Run by Captain **Leesis Estromyl**, an elf, the Jade District Watch has several somewhat conflicting reputations. Among most residents of the Jade District, their neighborhood's watch are upstanding, proper citizens, heroes of justice, and generally about as excellent of people as commoners can possibly hope to be. Some even come from well-to-do families. Among the poor of Cat's Cradle, by contrast, the Jade District Watch has a reputation for heavy-handedness, brutal bias against the poor, no interest in justice whatsoever, and general snobbery.

Finally, among the watch in other parts of Cat's Cradle, the reputation of the Jade District branch is that of lazy louts who let private security do most of their work for them and then take credit for their district's "clean, safe" streets in order to lord it over other watch houses. There are also rumors of corruption and bribe-taking among "the greens," as is their nickname among non-Jade District watch members. Even Baron Scale has expressed concern over Captain Estromyl's membership and participation in the Officers' Club (**Location J-15**), but Estromyl has repeatedly asserted that he would never let anything come between him and his duty to uphold the law in Cat's Cradle.

Adventure Hook: A radical political group is tired of the way the security forces hired in the Jade District are running roughshod over poor people. They want to hire some likeminded characters to deliver a kick in the teeth to one of these gangs of supposed law enforcers," in particular one known as the "Night-Street Watchers" that operates essentially like a criminal gang. J-10. Jade Square

Often considered the moral heart of the Jade District, Jade Square is known for establishments dedicated to dignity, grace, and general propriety. Lady Gwynlinn's Reading Room and the Officers' Club are located here, near the illustrious Neville Mansion and the Branlith Conservatory. On the opposite end of the Jade Square neighborhood, halfway between the square and the Coldwater Finishing School, stand several decorous boarding houses for unmarried servants and commoner attendees at Coldwater. These are dedicated to ensuring boarders' virtue and a lack of embarrassing scandals.

Rumors fly fast in the Jade Square neighborhood, and everyone pays minute attention to everyone else's every flaw. Of course, the richer one is, the more of a blind eye even Jade Square gossips might be willing to turn, but gods help any ordinary citizen accused of impropriety while living near Jade Square.

J–11. Lady Gwynlinn's Reading Room

Lady Gwynlinn's Reading Room is an exclusive library with a high membership fee. Each member may bring one guest at a time, but the Reading Room properties are not permitted to leave the premises. No children or pets are permitted, as they might damage the books or furniture.

The Reading Room is cleverly designed to be especially quiet inside and is full of private-seeming nooks, plush furnishings, and a wide selection of books from all over the world. Many are illuminated manuscripts or otherwise works of art in themselves. There is a strong emphasis on poetry and philosophy, but the odd example of a work from any subject can be found here.

Lady Gwynlinn is herself present in the mornings and afternoons on about half of all days (at random) and is quite knowledgeable about her collection. Her servants, **Essa** and **Bren**, are similarly knowledgeable, and make tea and serve light snacks for members and their guests if desired. Either Essa or Bren is always present if the Reading Room is open, which it usually is every morning and afternoon.

In the evenings, Lady Gwynlinn sometimes uses her Reading Room for private discussion groups on various topics, and these are known to sometimes become quite political, advocating for such radical notions as voting for civic offices and parliamentary representation for commoners. The comportment of Lady Gwynlinn and her friends has thus far been sufficiently decorous as to not warrant any reprimand from their baron, despite their potentially seditious ideas.

Adventure Hook: Someone connected with the Reading Room puts the characters into contact with the town's radical political underground (see **Radical Politics** in the introduction).

J-12. THE MARKET OF PROMISES

Located near the Panhandle District as well as one of the two public bridges across the Quicksilver, the Market of Promises is the place where the general public is grudgingly permitted to do business in the Jade District. All manner of shops and boutiques are located here and cater to the wealthy Jade District residents, but are willing to show off to the city's other citizens (and sometimes even deign to accept their money).

The most currently famous shops in the Promises neighborhood are Drello's Fine Garments, the All Your Promises jeweler, and the recently established Horizon's Promise art gallery. All three are especially difficult to access for the average customer however, and other jewelers, clothiers, art- and trinket-dealers, and so forth, are much more welcoming to the general public.

Many Market of Promises' shops have adopted a tradition (started by the All Your Promises owner, Celesa Tolban) of using the word "promise" in their names, though the Market of Promises gained its moniker long before this fad took hold, as it was known as a place that promised glorious finery, while charging through the nose for its goods, as well as a place where one purchased the means to make one's shallow promises more believable. (There is, after all, nothing like a well-set gemstone to make a romantic lie seem sincere.)

J-13. THE MASON'S GUILD

Near the heart of the Jade District stands a wedge-shaped structure of particular elegance. This is the new Mason's Guild house, built during the first scramble of Cat's Cradle's elite to abandon the crumbling Old City. The guild history, preserved in busts of the current and previous guildmasters, is oddly short for so old and masonry-influenced a city as Cat's Cradle. The guild library is similarly uncontaminated by records of the masonry families most associated with the "ripplestone" era of Cat's Cradle's history.

Though the conspicuous absence of records makes it difficult to determine exactly how this was accomplished, the Cat's Cradle Mason's Guild appears to have lost little to no face over the ripplestone debacle that still scars the city's streets. Local mason families tend to be wealthy and respected, with as many apprentices as they can wish for, and the Mason's Guild building is well-appointed and always busy. **Charma Stonesmen**, the current guildmaster, is said to be especially influential, a personal friend of both the baron's mother and Lady Neville, the socialite's socialite. **Adventure Hook:** An inventor named Thesper Janticleer recently approached the masons with a machine that measures seismic movements, proposing that it could be used to avoid minor foundation damage to buildings. The masons agreed to experiment with it and have been taking readings from various spots in the city. However, the readings have been consistently building up, and the masons realized that something is building up to create an artificial earthquake in the city. Time might be very short to discover the source.

J-14. THE NEVILLE MANSION

Located near Jade Square, the Neville Mansion is neither the largest nor the loveliest of the city's private homes, but it is inarguably the best-designed for throwing balls. All the grandest private parties in Cat's Cradle take place in the Neville family home, whose current matriarch, Lady Neville, is widely seen as the most elegant and wittiest socialite the city has ever seen.

Though minor, landless aristocrats, the Neville family matriarch or patriarch is granted the right to inherit the title of lord or lady from generation to generation, so long as the local baron does not choose to withdraw their status. The Nevilles have invested wisely over the centuries and are quite wealthy, so it is understood that barons of Cat's Cradle tend to need the Nevilles' goodwill in order to effectively govern, thus securing the family's landless title through the decades.

The current Lady Neville is unmarried and childless and is said to have refused thousands of marriage proposals in her life. She remains quite beautiful

for her 60 years, and is as charming and sharp of wit as ever. Her current heir is her nephew, Grenten Neville, a bookish young man of dashing good looks who is known for his satirical poetry. He and his aunt are alike and different in just the right ways to make them detest one another, but she has taken no action to impede his legal status as her heir, though they notably avoid one another at her parties.

Adventure Hook: Neville Mansion parties are among the best places to gather information among Cat's Cradle's wealthy, especially as they are known for free-flowing wine and just *slightly* loose morals. The characters are offered invitations to a party — they are forgeries, but very good ones — and the forger is selling them for a very low price.

J-15. THE OFFICERS' CLUB

The Officers' Club is a comfortable meeting house for anyone both invited to join and able to afford membership. Its interior is well-appointed and well-staffed, always stocked with delicious food, and offers fine sets of a number of games of chance and skill, so long as one can play them in a quiet and dignified manner. Private rooms are also available, and no questions are asked or answered about what goes on inside them.

A member may bring one guest at a time, but only upper military officers, captains of ships above a certain crew size, and persons of aristocratic bloodlines are ever invited to become members themselves. Anyone may join, so long as they are of sufficient "quality."

Despite many overt similarities of purpose shared between the Officers' Club and Lady Gwynlinn's Reading Room, the two organizations' reputations are not similar at all. While both are snobby and understood to be out of touch with the needs of ordinary folk, the Officers' Club is seen as the far more sinister of the two, always swirling with rumors of conspiracies to disenfranchise poorer businesspeople, or even worse crimes. One persistent rumor is that dead bodies are removed by the servants' entrance as often as two or three times a year.

While the Baronial Constabulary (see **Location D-1**) is said to have an eye on the place, thus far no specific charges have been brought to the baron. It is speculated that Officers' Club members are too influential to be touched by the law.

Adventure Hook: A minor priest at the Temple of Sefagreth (**Location G-16**) has just received absolute proof that a shopkeeper was murdered in order to get his small business out of the way of one of his competitors. The trail leads to some kind of deal made at the Officers' Club, and the body might even be in the basement there.

J-16. PIKE SQUARE

Named for its central jade-marble statue of General Pike, a minor aristocrat from Cat's Cradle who achieved a certain degree of fame in a far-off military conflict generations ago, the Pike Square neighborhood of Cat's Cradle's Jade District is known for such stuffy "rich people" enterprises as Fethen Bank and Investment, other investors' offices, several expensive barristers, and the offices of the city's two wealthiest shipping families (though both also have less-fancy offices near their berths on the docks).

Quiet and heavily guarded, mostly by Fethen family private security, Pike Square is sometimes described as the single dullest neighborhood in all of Cat's Cradle, and also the safest. Naturally, only the best and subtlest of pickpockets dare to work the Pike Square streets.

J-17. THE TEMPLE OF PROSPERITY

Constructed primarily of the local jade-marble, this grandiose, colonaded structure is elegant and gaudy, graceful and excessive at once. Rich with gilded flourishes and pompous sculpture, the Temple of Prosperity is arguably the most beautiful (or most embarrassing) edifice in Cat's Cradle. It is dedicated to various popular deities of agriculture, commerce, and local industries like masonry, brick-making, fishing, and alchemy, and is the largest building in the Jade District.

Catering to the city's wealthy, more than to public piety, the Temple of Prosperity doubles as a theater for the entertainment of the city's elite, even charging admission to some of its grander pageants (so as to keep the rabble away). At night, this is a gathering place for local and visiting bigwigs, ever drenched in such glamour as can be procured in so isolated a city. Priests of this temple are known more for their wealth and influence than for such priestly behavior as caring for the populace or building community.

During daylight hours, clerical spells can be purchased here at great expense and with few questions asked, though petitioners must be dressed "respectfully" (in other words, must not look too poor) to be allowed into

the inner sanctuaries where such transactions take place. There, the most experienced priests take turns putting on a show of keeping beautiful candles lit, incenses burning, and of anointing sacred statues with expensive oils in highly choreographed rituals.

J-18. Tulixia's

The finest public bath in Cat's Cradle, Tulixia's bathing pools are always clean, always hot, and never smoky, with a well-designed and efficient heating system. Business deals of all kinds are negotiated here.

J-19. Uiregard's Enchantments

In the northern Jade District, just off Oddwater Way, stands a plain door with a fine but simple sign reading Uiregard's Enchantments. This is the storefront of a wizard for hire. He charges exorbitant prices for his work, but he is honest, charming, quite normal as wizards go, and has an excellent professional reputation. In the Jade District, people generally feel that one gets what one pays for, and that Uiregard's work is worth the extra cost.

A well-dressed and handsome man in his 50s, **Uiregard** is courteous, soft-spoken, and easy to communicate with. He prefers to deal in items and potions, which he makes in his workshop in the back, but he is also sometimes willing to offer other sorts of spellcasting, by appointment only, in other parts of the city (with additional fees for his travel time). Uiregard's spellbook is quite extensive, and he allows other wizards to copy spells from it for similarly exorbitant rates.

Uiregard keeps a very ordinary secretary to do his bookkeeping and keep track of his appointments. He is often booked several weeks in advance. He does not take apprentices.

J-20. The Westside Courthouse

The Westside Courthouse is located in Pike Square across from Fethen Bank and Investment and behind the Baronial Mansion. After moving his family from Cat's Keep to the Jade District, old Baron Scolren decided he wanted to govern from the Jade District as well and began construction on the Westside Courthouse. It was not completed in his lifetime, but his daughter,

Baroness Escaulla, and her son, Baron Escallel (Baron Scale's father), both used this grand (and rather impractically laid-out) edifice as their primary seat of governance, outside certain traditional annual events.

Baron Scale, however, prefers to make himself more accessible to the common people and has thus restored his courthouse to the old, drafty audience hall inside the walls of Cat's Keep, far more centrally located for all of Cat's Cradle's citizenry. Since this move on his part, the Westside Courthouse has continued operation, but only for routine legal matters such as recordkeeping, witnessing of contracts, and such minor disputes as do not require the baron's personal attention.

The wealthy of the Jade District are generally displeased by this change of policy, but in truth their courthouse continues to provide them with much greater legal convenience than is enjoyed by any other part of the city, as contracts, new businesses, wills, and other paperwork is processed far more quickly for Jade District residents than any other neighborhood.

Adventure Hook: One of the clerks at the courthouse was recently called upon to witness and record a contract. He realized only afterward that he had been looking at an agreement to commit murder, but when he pulled the file the contract had disappeared. He and his superiors are now concerned, but all they have to work with is the description of the two men who signed the contract … and one of them looked a great deal like the dead Baron Escallel.

J-21. Wythys and Daughter

The best-regarded apothecary in the Jade District is the shop of Wythys and Daughter, located in the Pouch of Coins neighborhood. Run out of their small but posh home, the enterprise is — like most shops in the Jade District — expensive and rather exclusive, catering to wealthy, regular customers. Sara and Dala Wythys are excellent apothecaries, in their way, dealing in high-quality herbs, poultices, and medicinal alchemy, as well as similar products.

With the help of a few servants, the mother and daughter proprietors grow their own herbs wherever possible for the climate and import quality dried ingredients where necessary. They are also skilled alchemists, though neither is well-traveled, and both prefer to work in herbs and medicines.

Though sweet of disposition and probably well-intentioned, the Wythys' are not above a bit of con-artistry in meeting their customers' needs. They brew no harmful medicines, but some of their expensive concoctions have no effect whatsoever and are useful only as placebos. Others are mildly intoxicating.

THE OLD CITY

Once the domain of Cat's Cradle's elite, the Old City, stretching downward from the southeastern walls of the keep almost to the Docks neighborhood, was formerly the pride of Cat's Cradle. Though not really older than parts of the Gold District or Bricktown, the Old City does contain most of Cat's Cradle's oldest mansions, temples, and other grand structures. These are constructed, almost exclusively, of a beautiful marbled-brown stone, unique to this region, known as ripplestone. In appearance, it resembles something between petrified wood and a marbled steak, and visitors often remark upon its loveliness and upon the skillful architecture of the neighborhood as a whole.

Unfortunately, ripplestone is not a stable building material and begins to crumble and dissolve in the elements after only a century or so of exposure to the mild local weather — wearing out faster than well-cared-for wood and being significantly more difficult to repair. Local alchemists love to pontificate about how alchemical testing before construction could have prevented the Old City's tragedy, but Cat's Cradle's alchemy boom had not yet begun at the time. The oldest of Cat's Cradle's mason families was deeply disgraced by the ripplestone debacle (and have been erased from the Masons Guild records), but the damage was already done.

Thus, grand though they once were, many buildings in the Old City are crumbling and unusable, dangerous even to enter. Others are propped up with mismatched repairs in brick or wood. For safety reasons (and to reclaim useful acreage), the barons of Cat's Cradle regularly budget city funds for tearing down some beautiful ruin or other, to be replaced with simpler construction, but teardown projects tend to be expensive and dangerous given how unpredictable ripplestone's disintegration can be. As such, many dangerous old structures still stand, and some are even occupied by those with nowhere else to go.

Everyone who can leave the Old City to move to the Jade or Gold districts has done so long ago, and despite the bedraggled grandeur of the remaining architecture — and even the occasional sculpture garden — this has become a very poor district, home to criminal operations, social outcasts, and very little industry.

O-1. THE CENTAUR

At the end of the street now known as Ingrate's Walk stands a pedestaled ripplestone statue, one of the two most prominent of such slowly melting monuments in the Old City. This particular larger-than-life statue was originally a horse and rider, and students of the city's history can even explain how this same "rider" was also the unwitting source of the name of Ingrate's Walk.

These days, however, the average Old City resident knows the dilapidated monument only as "The Centaur." Once a man leaning forward on a horse, the horse's head broke off ages ago, as did the man's raised sword arm. The decapitated horse head is now a mostly shapeless boulder lying a few yards away from the statue, which has itself lost most of its shape. It does vaguely resemble a child's clumsy clay rendition of a centaur, though it is believed that soon the rest of the rider will break off from the top of the statue, and the remains of the horse will become an indistinguishable lump atop the bronze pedestal.

The Centaur is known as a place to avoid in the Old City, especially after dark, as it is said to be one of the several regular meeting places of the Cat's Cradle Thieves' Guild.

O-2. THE DOGS

A partial ruin known as the Dogs stands just southwest of the Old Temple and right at the wall between the Old City and the Docks. Once the fortress-like mansion of a retired knight, the Dogs was only partially built of ripplestone and has been shored up in a shabby and precarious-looking manner with mismatched scrap wood and other cheaply acquired materials. The end result is a rambling 12-foot-high outer wall encompassing an oddly shaped and only partially roofed interior.

Inside, the Dogs is filthy, not particularly furnished, and smells like the majority of its inhabitants: dozens of stray dogs. They may originally have been strays, but the Dogs' dogs are surprisingly well-trained in the services of a strange woman named Dru. Dru's dogs appear to obey her every command, and gods help anyone attempting to enter her domain without her permission.

Dru takes in and cares for any stray dogs she finds and is rumored to even possess some healing ability (which she uses exclusively on her dogs, it seems). She is rude and monosyllabic with anyone who isn't a canine, and all manner of rumors circulate as to where she gets the meat to feed her four-pawed army. She is known to work with several information brokers of varying reputations and seems somehow to maintain a working relationship with the Kennocks and the watch.

Adventure Hook: A wizard visiting the town has a bottled manticore that needs to be let out at night to feed. It is trained not to attack people unless the wizard tells it to do so, and ordinarily it preys on dogs. It discovered Dru's dogs and killed several of them. Dru wants the characters to find the monster killing her dogs and slay it. She has some interesting information about developments in the city that she can offer them in payment.

O-3. THE HAUNTED LADY

The Haunted Lady is the second most prominent of the two slowly melting ripplestone statues in the Old City. Originally sculpted with a hair-veil and flowing robe of marble, such that only her face and limbs were made of ripplestone, the Haunted Lady has crumbled in a remarkable way.

Her robe and veil remain beautiful, but the space under her semi-revealing raiment, where her legs once showed, is now an open hollow. Her arms, once clasped at her heart, are now a half-dissolved mess, dripping down over her marble breast. Eeriest of all, the signature brown ripples of the ripplestone, once said to have given her a sweet, sorrowful expression, have dissolved to make her face now resemble a skull.

Located only a few blocks south of Saint Kada's, the Haunted Lady has become an object of strange and fearful worship by Old City orphans and street children. Her pedestal is often covered in humble offerings, and the tiny hollow beneath her marble skirts is often filled by a homeless child's camp, as Saint Kada's beds are often far too full.

O-4. HOLLAM'S

No one gets sick in Cat's Cradle, but people still become injured or sometimes poisoned, and the poor of the Old City can't always afford to visit a temple for healing. For these, there is Hollam's. Hollam Westtrel is an old man with a mysterious past who lives in the Old City for reasons he does not disclose. Some decades ago, word got out that he could treat poisons and injuries, and he has taken up the role of a doctor ever since, treating anyone who comes to him as best he can, and charging no more than his patients can afford.

Hollam knows little magic and does not speak of religion, but he does seem to be a cleric of some kind, if not a very good one. He is, however, far more skilled at nonmagical healing, with a gentle and patient manner, with a gift for minimizing scars with his stitches. He can be found in a small stone hut (formerly a private stables) not far north of the Old Temple.

Hollam helps anyone who needs him, no questions asked, even Kennock's crew. He charges so little that he himself lives hand-to-mouth, but the people of the Old City bring him food and supplies on a regular basis, and he never asks where such gifts come from — merely accepts them and puts them to use in healing those in need. It is said that anyone who harms Hollam Westtrel faces swift retribution from any number of Old City residents.

Adventure Hook: Hollam's past has caught up with him, and a small band of mercenaries he ran with in times gone by has kidnapped him. Unbeknownst to the kidnappers, they raised a hornets' nest. The Thieves' Guild and other groups post a substantial reward for Hollam's safe return.

O-5. KENNOCK'S PLACE

The Kennock family have lived in the Cat's Cradle region since time immemorial and were wealthy landowners for most of that span. At around the time of the ripplestone exodus, however, it so happened that the Kennock family was in disgrace, with its patriarch imprisoned in the keep's tower and its titles and most of its ancestral holdings stripped away.

The Kennock family was permitted to retain its rights to its Old City mansion, which as luck would have it, was constructed without ripplestone. The ruined minor aristocrats chose not to spend the last of their fortune on following the rest of Cat's Cradle's elite to the Jade District and instead remained in the Old City to see how they could take advantage of the power vacuum left behind.

In the generations since, the Kennock name has sunk ever further into the city's worst muck, but the Kennock family has nevertheless become, in its own way, more powerful than ever. Not many understand the complex political and financial intrigues that conspire to make the current "Old Kennock" untouchable by the law, but she lives in her ancestral mansion like a tyrant of old, and is treated by most in her district as if her word might carry more weight than even that of the baron.

No illegal activity takes place at or near the Kennock household, and Old Kennock, though in height and breadth she resembles a cross between a bear and a barbarian queen, maintains a dignified demeanor and impeccable wardrobe, just as if her family were still aristocrats. Everyone knows that the Kennock Syndicate criminal organization answers to her personally, but one would never know it from the upright and proper state of her home.

Her vast army of younger siblings, children, nieces, nephews, cousins, and a few "retired" aunts and uncles maintain similar decorum when "at home," but range throughout the Old City in their activities and "business concerns." Elsewhere, they are not always, as it were, on their best behavior.

O-6. Madame Olella's

Out at the western edge of the Old City stands a strangely lovely example of mismatched repairs on a ripplestone structure. Something about the way the walls crumbled, combined with the granite, brick, and wood used to shore up the damage makes for a beautiful chimera of a rambling mansion. This is Madame Olella's, the best-known brothel in Cat's Cradle. Complex agreements between the Kennocks, the Gold District watch, and various key power players in the city ensure that Madame Olella's is a basically legal establishment.

Madame Olella is believed to have strong ties to the Thieves' Guild, but to nevertheless be a force for stability and nonviolence in the Old City district. That said, those who mistreat Madame Olella or her staff tend to face severe repercussions from Olella's allies.

O-7. Niftin's Knick Knacks

Located near the Rat Market and often considered to be an extension of it is a rickety wooden shack of a shop, built inside the fallen ruins of a larger, mostly missing ripplestone structure. This is Niftin's Knick Knacks. Inside can be found fake magic items, cheap brass jewelry with paste gemstones being sold at just under real gem prices, "foreign treasures" of suspicious veracity, various pawned trinkets, badly carved ripplestone figurines (Niftin's own

work), and occasionally stolen goods.

Niftin himself is a compulsive liar of surprising charm, though he tends to resemble a cross between a yshkat and a bag of filthy rags. He seems to take great pleasure in cheating his customers and is known to overcharge or underpay for goods at every opportunity, yet he does so in such an entertaining manner, full of wild tales and cunning humor, that most customers leave surprisingly satisfied. His shop is a cluttered mess full of dust, cobwebs, and scruffy feral cats.

All that said, however, Niftin sometimes comes into possession of something worth a great deal more than he realizes, and it is not unheard of for real magic items (or cursed ones) to be found among his piles of interesting trash.

Adventure Hook: Niftin comes into possession of a powerful magic item and finds himself in the middle of three different factions that want to steal it — even if they have to kill Niftin in the process. Niftin, more interested than they are in his survival, hires the adventurers to keep him safe and to resolve the issue, possibly by staging their own theft of the object so Niftin is no longer at risk.

O-8. The Old Hospital

A wedge-shaped building in the heart of the Old City, just where Ingrate's Walk meets the Centaur's square, was once a grand public hospital, open even to the poor. Built back when disease could still happen in Cat's Cradle, it was part of a philanthropic vogue that washed through Cat's Cradle's elite a few centuries ago.

The hospital is, as such, possibly the oldest building in the Old City neighborhood, predating the discovery of the now-abandoned ripplestone quarry. As such, its foundations are strong, and its outer walls still quite stable. Nevertheless, it stands emptier than even some of the more dangerous ruins around it and has for most of its existence. City records show that every few generations someone decides to do something new with the old hospital. It has been an inn, a school, an upscale brothel, a con artist's house of wonders, and more, but none of these enterprises has ever lasted more than a few years, and all have ended in apparently unrelated disaster and tragedy (including but not limited to fire, flood, freak accidents, and murder).

It is believed that the Thieves' Guild is currently making some secret use of the Old Hospital, but sane and reasonable people avoid the place.

Adventure Hook: The baron has offered a reward to any who can discover what ails this perfectly repairable and usable old building, but all attempts thus far have turned out to be chicanery and nonsense (or, at least, have failed to convince Baron Scale of their veracity). The true source of the Old Hospital's apparent curse remains a mystery.

O-9. THE OLD TEMPLE

About halfway between the Plaza and the Haunted Lady stands one of the largest ruins in the Old City. This is the Old Temple, once the religious heart of Cat's Cradle. Built entirely of ripplestone in an intricate and lovely design, the Old Temple's disintegration with the passage of time has been a particular mess. More than most structures, the Old Temple was constructed in a way that is difficult to shore up due to its design and its great size. It is also difficult to dismantle due to the complexity of its many advanced structural techniques. Short of hiring teams of wizards to take the place down by *levitation* (an expense beyond even the baron's coffers), it is difficult to organize a safe means of removing this perilous ruin from the Old City streets.

Taking into account that, even as it crumbles, the Old Temple remains terribly beautiful, with a sorrowful majesty to its slowly dissolving stonework — and also that this was once a place of worship and serenity remembered for uplifting song and for far more piety than the fancy new Temple of Prosperity in the Jade District — and the residents of Cat's Cradle have found there to be little *will* to dismantle the Old Temple, no matter how dangerous its failing grandeur may have become.

Indeed, it seems increasingly likely that some terrible accident will have to occur before action is taken. In the meantime, the Old Temple is a place, however precarious it may be, where those who have nowhere else to go are known to take shelter. By mute local agreement, no violence takes place there, and everyone understands that those humble offerings still left to the crumbling statues of the gods are fair game to any destitute enough to take up residence in so teetering an abode.

O-10. OX'S LABOR

Due south of the Rat Market, on the edge of the Docks neighborhood, stands a recent, dull brick construction proclaiming itself to be Ox's Labor. Ox was a stevedore who stumbled into some money and was able to acquire a ruin-strewn lot for cheap, building upon it an office and barracks-like dorm for what he hoped would be the perfect way to revitalize the Old City.

His intention was a place where solid workers down on their luck could enjoy a bed to sleep in and the benefits of Ox's networking services. Ox himself would then act as a go between for supplying workers to places that needed them, taking only a small cut for his efforts. He intended this to be a win for everyone: workers, employers, and himself all at once.

Unfortunately, Ox died in a construction accident after only a few years in business. Since his death, Ox's Labor has gone in a radically different direction than its founder intended. It is still a place where people with nowhere else to turn can go looking for work and a bed, but pay and conditions are universally terrible for those workers now known colloquially as "the oxen." According to rumor, many workers disappear from Ox's every year, some say to slave barges or worse.

The current proprietor, an "old friend" of Ox's named **Tral Zesser**, is believed to be a major figure in the Thieves' Guild and possibly a rival of the Kennocks.

Adventure Hook: The Kennock Syndicate (or one of its factions) approaches the characters about removing Tral from his position and making him disappear somewhere.

O-11. THE PLAZA

Deep in the southern Old City stands a monument to the first baron and founder of Cat's Keep. With a pedestal and roof of granite, the ripplestone statue within remains in excellent condition and depicts a stout-shouldered and bearded human in fanciful "historical" garb and armaments. The figure is bending down from its rocky perch to help up a fellow human, a yshkat, and a dwarven child, symbolizing the legend that the first baron brought peace and prosperity to the former residents of the region. The area around this statue has been called the Plaza for many generations and is one of the few places in the Old City to retain its former name since the ripplestone exodus.

There is constant talk of moving this statue away from the crime-ridden Old City, but many Old City residents are quite attached to it, and the first baron (Baron Orshal) has become a folk hero and almost saint to many. Offerings of wildflowers, pretty stones, and humble little craft objects constantly decorate the base of the statue, and the neighborhood immediately around the Plaza is among the cleanest and safest in the Old City. Perhaps for this reason, no baron has yet approved a project to dismantle and relocate the founder's statue.

O-12. QUEEVES' CHICKENS

Queeves, a mononymous personage of indeterminate species and androgynous countenance (male-identified), keeps chickens. Lots of chickens. Occupying a large, fenced-off lot on the Plaza (which Queeves has somehow come to legally own, apparently), Queeves' Chickens includes a crumbled ruin, a small wooden hut, and a spacious and fancy brick chicken coop. There is also a wide yard guarded by a pair of well-trained mastiff mongrels, and otherwise full of happy, fat chickens.

Queeves himself is found at home with his chickens only during early morning and late evening feedings, as he spends most of his time hiking up and down the city with a cart full of today's fresh eggs. He delivers eggs to most locations in the Old City and in addition sells discounted chicken meat, though the latter is usually from an elderly bird and runs toward the tough and stringy. Queeves prefers to sell his meat to customers willing to hear out the names and life stories of the departed chickens they purchase. He appears to love and cherish each chicken individually.

In addition to his other quirks, Queeves seems to somehow know everyone in the Old City and everything that happens there. He will let some information slip in the course of conversation with anyone willing to listen to him ramble on about his chickens, but he is smart enough to charge money for any really useful or juicy facts.

O-13. THE RAT MARKET

This open square to the south of Cat's Keep was once a lovely little public garden called Cat's Corner. After the Old City fell into disrepair, however, the groundskeepers were assigned elsewhere, and the garden became an overgrown tangle. Only a few years later, Cat's Cradle's poorer districts became infested by a large and vicious breed of rats carried to the region on some barge or other (the precise source was never determined, only that it hit the docks first, and then the Old City).

Full as the district was with so many abandoned buildings, the rats grew truly out of control in the Old City, until eventually the town militia was mustered to clear out all untended vegetation to give the rats fewer food sources and places to hide. That was the end of Cat's Corner, and indeed, a vast swarm of rats was evicted from the destroyed garden. The ugly, dead remnants of the place came to be known as Rat's Corner instead.

Now that the Rat's Corner lot was clear of overgrown foliage, an enterprising few of the neighborhood's newer, poorer residents began setting up little shops in the open space, on blankets or in simple booths, selling trinkets, cheap or used goods, and similar. The Rat's Corner Market became a tradition, now shortened to just the Rat Market. These days, the Rat Market is quietly understood to be under the domain of the Kennock Syndicate and to be crawling with pickpockets. Some of the booths and blankets sell items of quite questionable origin.

The town sewers are easily accessible from grates at the edges of the Rat Market and run down to the river from here. Upriver (or "upsewer," more technically) the sewer tunnels branch out and can be used by the brave or desperate to reach other parts of the city. These grates are occasionally used for disposal of bodies and can be used as a good jumping-off point for any adventure based in a town's sewers.

Adventure Hook: Five rat-men of some kind were recently observed climbing down into the sewers with what appeared to be a body wrapped in a blanket. The blanket was making muffled shouting sounds, so presumably a captive is somewhere down in the sewers.

O-14. SAINT KADA'S ORPHANAGE

Behind the Old Temple, out on the eastern edge of the Old City, where crumbling ripplestone meets the stout, simple brick of Bricktown, stands an ugly mishmash of a structure known as Saint Kada's Orphanage. Originally a school of fine art and sculpture, it was abandoned with the rest of the Old City and stood mostly empty for some time.

A few decades back, however, residents noticed that repairs were being made to the old building, with solid brick shoring up the most vital weak points and weather-sealed wood roofing or siding being added to protect the ripplestone beneath from further damage by sun and rain. When the watch looked into this unauthorized construction, it was discovered that a group of orphans had been stealing the means to rebuild their home from various brickyards, lumber barges, and other businesses throughout the city.

The orphans were led by a bright young woman named Kada, herself the orphaned daughter of a pair of trained architects. Kada insisted on taking full responsibility for all the crimes involved, to spare the other orphans. During her trial, several businesses retroactively "donated" their products to the rebuilding efforts, and the baron officially designated the now-ugly-but-sound building as an orphanage. However, some businessowners remained enraged by the theft, and Kada was ultimately sent to prison to work off the debt of all she'd stolen.

Between her own years of hard prison labor and a number of anonymous donations, her debt was paid nine years ago, and Kada is now free to once more manage her orphanage herself. Despite her hard treatment by the law, Kada remains a kind and stubborn woman, and most who meet her understand why "Saint Kada" has become her nickname.

Adventure Hook: A cleric in the party keeps having visions of the orphanage, and when it is finally located, Saint Kada considers their appearance to be tremendously lucky, for five of her children disappeared last night (long after the cleric's visions began). She believes that the children saw or overheard some kind of discussion they shouldn't have, and that they might be in terrible danger from the Kennock Syndicate or some other criminal group … or possibly even corrupt members of the city watch.

O-15. Shevekka's

Shevekka looks human, though rumor makes her out to be almost anything else. She looks to be of attractive middle age, though rumor would make her centuries old and possibly undead. What appearance and rumor agree upon, however, is that Shevekka is a wizard for hire who keeps offices in the Old City district of Cat's Cradle, in what was once the gardener's shed for a now long-demolished mansion.

Why a capable wizard would maintain so small and humble an abode is unknown, but as she also does not advertise her services, nor even mark her place of business with a sign on the door, some have suggested that when she relocated to Cat's Cradle some decades ago, she was going into hiding to avoid an enemy or the consequences of some crime.

But few know much for certain about Shevekka the wizard. She is said to be willing to do anything for money (or sufficiently valuable trade), no questions asked. She is said to have no moral compass and to be quite dangerous to approach without proper courtesy. While the Baronial Constabulary do keep an eye on her, however, she has yet to be convicted of a crime by any Cat's Cradle official.

Adventure Hook: Shevekka has received a dangerous commission to produce a magic item for an unknown patron willing to pay well. However, she needs materials — very specific ones — from the Salchamp mines north of the city.

O-16. Syl's Odd Jobs

Not far from the Rat Market stand the dull and simple offices of Syl's Odd Jobs. Syl is an elf, although he avoids mention of his family and ancestry. He has lived in Cat's Cradle his whole life (well over a century), and for the last several decades has made a somewhat lazy excuse for a modest living by performing odd jobs for anyone willing to hire him.

Syl seems to be skilled in almost every vocation, or is at least able to fake it well, and he also maintains a network of skilled friends to call upon when his own abilities are not up to a task. He and his eclectic companions present a somewhat bored and selfish appearance to the world, but rumor makes them out to be much, much more. Not only do some say that Syl's Odd Jobs will work for free if the cause is good (passionately denied by Syl), but the deeper rumor is that Syl and his friends are secretly city-based adventurers and more useful than the watch when trouble threatens Cat's Cradle's Old City.

O-17. The Thieves' Guild

There is no physical location in Cat's Cradle called a Thieves' Guild, but the presence of the Thieves' Guild is felt throughout the Old City and is considered by many residents to be the most important authority in the district. Some believe the Thieves' Guild to be simply another term for the Kennock Syndicate, but most assume "the Guild" to be a districtwide conspiracy of extra-legal "authority" figures coordinating activities to their mutual benefit.

Other than Old Kennock, who is variously assumed to be either the leader or the muscle of the organization, Guild leaders are believed to include Tral Zesser of Ox's Labor, Jondret Boon of the Upper Crust Inn, possibly Madame Olella, probably some unknown corrupt watch officer, and other sometimes fanciful postulations such as Shevekka the wizard, various unpopular rich people from other parts of the city, a secret cadre of trained spy-assassins, and of course any number of literal fiends, and even the mysterious lake monster.

Whatever its membership, the Thieves' Guild is understood to meet in secret every few weeks at rotating locations (mostly — but not exclusively — within the Old City), to determine the upcoming course of criminal activity throughout Cat's Cradle. It is also understood that one does not set up shop in the western Old City without Thieves' Guild permission (usually obtained through the Kennock Syndicate). Individual criminals caught and interrogated by the Baronial Constabulary only know their immediate bosses, but all claim to believe that said bosses, even Kennock, answer to the Guild, about which captured criminals have always known little.

Those who have angered the Thieves' Guild have, on occasion, told tales of being kidnapped with sacks over their heads, dragged to an unknown location, interrogated by a circle of distorted voices, and set free after agreeing to whatever the Guild demanded. It is assumed that those who fail to agree to the Guild's terms do not return from such an adventure.

O-18. Treesa's Pub

Hailed by its regulars as the best pub in the Old City, Treesa's is a homey little establishment recently and sturdily constructed near the Plaza. **Treesa** is a human who grew up in Cat's Cradle's Old City, achieved humble success as a soldier and adventurer in the wide world, and decided a life of violence wasn't for her. She brought her modest wealth home with her and used it to start her small pub, in a desire to be part of the rebuilding of the Old City.

While Treesa's own combat prowess is sufficient to deal with run-of-the-mill disturbances in her pub, she prefers to keep a low profile in order to avoid trouble with the Kennocks or the Thieves' Guild. As such, her premises are small and simple, and occasionally crowded. Treesa's beer and food are good, though hardly haute cuisine, and she keeps no expensive spirits or goods on hand. She is known to be a sympathetic bartender, good with advice and even mediation of disputes.

O-19. The Upper Crust Inn

Jondret Boon, the self-proclaimed "best innkeeper in Cat's Cradle," runs a seedy establishment whose door signage euphemistically names it, "The Upper Crust Inn." This flea-bitten, rat-infested inn offers tiny rooms whose straw mattresses are never changed as often as any customers would like. Room rates are low, but guests' reports of the inn's quality are even lower, describing such amenities as sour, watered-down beer, unidentifiable meats, and stale or even moldy bread.

Though Boon claims otherwise, the Upper Crust's back room, available for private reservation, is also rumored to be one of the meeting places of the Cat's Cradle Thieves' Guild. Indeed, Boon himself is rumored to be a member. It is certainly true that his regulars in the inn's front common room do come across as a gang of dangerous goons. These are also treated to better ale and spirits than newer customers are typically served.

O-20. Abandoned Tenement

This is a three-story building that — on first inspection — appears to be structurally unsound, and dangerously so. A rough wooden sign reads, "Condemned by order of the Baron. Do not enter." The building is actually in much better shape than it appears, and it is rented out by its owner, **Oyad Thern**, to anyone who needs a large and inconspicuous place to work for a month or two. Needless to say, most of those who rent the building are using it for illegal purposes such as fencing operations, illegal magical or alchemical research, and other such activities. The building is referenced in the adventure module *The Eye of Itral*, but if you aren't running that adventure, the occupants from *The Eye of Itral* will have moved on (or not arrived yet) and you can use it either as an "abandoned" building or as a place the characters could rent if they make contact with Oyad Thern via any of the town's various illegal organizations. Oyad himself is not associated with any of these groups — he works with anyone for the right price, which happens to be 500 gp per month.

Adventure Hook: Oyad has agreed to rent the building to an anonymous tenant, as per usual, but he has become convinced that whoever the tenant is, they plan to kill him soon as a way of making sure no one can trace their activities back to them. He wants the characters to find out the tenant's identity and protect him from any kind of assassination attempt.

O-21. Temple of Ceres

The goddess Ceres is the Goddess of the Home and Midwives, Goddess of Healing, Mercy, and Patience. This three-story temple houses a chapel on the ground floor and contains the quarters of the priestesses on the upper floors.

The chapel's main feature is a large millstone in the center of the room (the millstone being the main symbol of the goddess). The chapel has been located here since before the decline of the Old City, and was not — probably due to divine intervention — affected by the physical deterioration of the buildings in this part of the town. The priestesses perform their mission throughout the town rather than just in the Old City, so the temple can easily be used for adventure hooks directed at adventurers of higher moral persuasion.

O-22. The Ragged Man's Warehouse

This warehouse is generally used as a storage place for street vendors and smaller merchants of the Old City and Dancer's Road. It is operated by an individual known as the Ragged Man, who dresses in ostentatiously rich — but old and threadbare — garments. The warehouse is well guarded, and the guards have a pack of three dogs. They check around the outside of the building on an hourly basis during the night.

THE PANHANDLE

This newest portion of the city was laid out a century ago after fire destroyed the Docks and baronial decree limited alchemical shipments to predesignated areas. Newer and better-protected docks were built in this area south of the Jade District, designed to receive and handle alchemical supplies and hazardous materials. Today, the Panhandle is almost its own city, separate from the rest of Cat's Cradle and home to its own governor, administration, and civic structure.

P-1. Jade Gate

The portal to and from the city's wealthiest district, the Jade Gate is made of granite faced with locally quarried jade marble. A vital pathway between the two important districts, the gate is constantly guarded by impeccably uniformed city watch members who make a great show of carefully inspecting cargo passing through. In reality, the guards usually only make cursory examinations and usually simply wave through cargoes from well-known individuals or businesses.

P-2. Baronial Records and Legal Offices

This sprawling structure sandwiched between the city wall and the Shipping Warehouse serves the barony as a repository for the ever-growing mass of law books, receipts, manifests, bills of lading, certifications, licenses and other bureaucratic records, and is managed by baronial chief documentarian **Isalk Dar** and several assistants. Records are stored on tall, tottering shelves organized more-or-less chronologically, with older records bound into binders or leather books and buried increasingly deeper in the archive. Isalk and his clerks are intimately familiar with the maze of shelves and papers and are known for their ability to locate records from almost any point in Cat's Cradle's history

The huge building serves a secondary purpose as containing offices of a number of legal solicitors who specialize in local law regarding trade, manufacture, taxes and transportation. This location, conveniently close to the records office, is ideal for those legal workers who need to constantly refer to documents for precedent and past transactions. These attorneys are generally oriented toward business matters such as settling disputes between merchants, helping to deal with fees and criminal charges from the barony, etc., but many are open to taking on other cases if the price is right, including criminal defense and representation of adventurers in their various disputes. Most of the solicitors here are familiar sights at the City Courthouse in Cat's Keep.

Adventure Hook: One of the attorneys needs to get the testimony of someone who is located in a dangerous place (Old City or the Warrens at **Location G-19**). The person has disappeared, whether due to foul play or out of fear, and the attorney wants the characters to find them.

P-3. The Calico Cat

A popular Panhandle tavern, the Calico Cat occupies a central location in the district and hosts a diverse crowd from all across the district, as well as tourists and visitors from elsewhere in the city who want to soak up a little local color. Innkeeper **Gustov Mellarian** makes certain that his customers represent the district well and always provide an entertaining sight to other patrons, and to this end he goes so far as to offer discounts to Alchemists' Guild members, nobles, and prominent adventurers, using them as celebrity draws to attract sightseers. The inn is also popular with less prominent individuals, as local merchants, alchemists, and brokers favor the Cat's pleasant and private meeting rooms for conducting private business.

As an inn, the Calico Cat is average at best, with basic but well-prepared fare and clean but ordinary rooms, though prices are somewhat higher than the Cat's counterparts in other sections of the city.

P-4. Alchemical Shipping Warehouse

This large and imposing structure serves dual purposes — as a warehouse for alchemical components and products awaiting outshipment, and as a protected dock facility for the offloading of hazardous materials. The lake-facing side of the structure opens onto a series of covered slips large enough to accommodate most local vessels, and each slip is reinforced and protected from the others by heavy stone walls. Vessels carrying volatile, explosive, corrosive, or flammable substances arrive and depart from these protected docks, overseen by representatives of the Alchemists' Guild and Cat's Cradle customs officers.

Elsewhere, alchemical goods are stored in long, sky-lit structures marked with seals and documents identifying their owners. The building's wide aisles are flanked by high shelves where packages and shipments of every size, shape, and description are kept, while light shines down through unbreakable alchemical ironglass skylights while human watch members, dwarven private security operatives, and a tireless squad of iron golems watch over them.

Adventure Hook: An open brawl in an area filled with explosives and iron golems is an opportunity not to be missed. Open mayhem is a rare opportunity for higher-level characters, and the Shipping Warehouse offers just that.

P-5. Panhandle Stables

Horses, wagons, and dray animals are in constant demand in Cat's Cradle, where they are employed to transport all forms of alchemical substances and to move cargo to and from warehouses and storage facilities. **Dageera Tashkheli** is a former nomad who transformed her skill with horse trading and breeding into a successful business here in the heart of the Panhandle. Mounts available through Tashkheli range from fine riding horses to powerful workhorses capable of towing enormous loads. Tashkheli supplements her business by selling carts and wagons as well, which she purchases from suppliers in the countryside.

P-6. Dexer's Rooming House

Dexer Harreaz manages this large tenement that he and several investors converted from a neglected multiple-use structure a decade or so ago. Rooms range from small and inexpensive to larger and more luxurious, and are occupied by various Panhandle working folk and more prosperous types who don't want or can't find a more permanent abode in the crowded district. Though Dexer makes a decent living from the building — good enough at least to maintain a luxury flat for himself, his wife, and his son — further digging into his carefully concealed finances might reveal stakes in Cat's Cradle gambling establishments and homes maintained for several mistresses, as well as connections to the Kennock Syndicate. All this sketchy high-living is financed by the rooming house's second, secret function — that of a secret alchemical lab where those with enough gold can concoct illicit substances safe from the prying eyes of the city watch or — worse — the constabulary.

The illicit labs are well hidden within the walls of the rooming house, and in several secret sub-cellars, accessible only through magically enhanced portals with passwords or arcane keys. Workspace varies from cramped to relatively roomy depending upon payments, and although the hidden rooms are reinforced and safe procedures are demanded from users, there is always a danger of spills, fires, and other accidents that might endanger other tenants. So far, all such accidents have been successfully contained or covered up, but future similar problems continue to worry Dexer.

Users are sworn to secrecy, and Dexer's contacts with the Kennock Syndicate have come in handy when he needs to dispose of tenants whom he considers to be "bad risks." So arrogant has he become, that one of his several mistresses was recently found murdered and floating down the River Hyon to the city watch's confusion and a decree of "accidental death" by investigators.

P-7. Nattwick's Clothiers

Halfling proprietor **Harthil Nattwick** and a staff of skilled tailors design and sell clothing of all sorts from his shop, but he specializes in protective gear and garments designed for use by alchemists, dockworkers, and others who handle hazardous materials. Nattwick's specialized garments incorporate various fabrics infused with chemical and alchemical substances that retard flames, reduce the effects of other elemental substances such as concentrated acids and bases, and can also provide some protection from cold, lightning, and even some arcane energies. Nattwick charges premium prices for these garments and though his customers are primarily alchemists and their employees, he also has a small but steady stream of adventurers among his clients, especially spellcasters who use his garments to protect them from hostile magic and elemental attack.

SUNDRY ROAD
Cat's Cradle
PANHANDLE
N
W
E
S
MAP P

Alchemy and Alchemical Products

Alchemy and arcane magic overlap in many important ways, and commonly known magical potions can be created using alchemical procedures. These are all available at alchemy businesses in Cat's Cradle, at prices as listed in the 5e core rules. Other non-arcane substances are available too, most notably antidotes and poisons, though the unlicensed sale of harmful or poisonous substances is strictly forbidden, and those vendors who do sell such items carefully investigate buyers and keep extensive records of all sales.

Various items include (see *Fortune Hunters* for details):
Candle of invocation, dust of disappearance, dust of dryness, dust of sneezing and choking, oil of etherealness, oil of sharpness, oil of slipperiness, philter of love, potion of animal friendship, potion of clairvoyance, potion of climbing, potion of diminution, potion of flying, potion of gaseous form, potion of hill giant strength, potion of frost giant strength, potion of stone giant strength, potion of fire giant strength, potion of cloud giant strength, potion of storm giant strength, potion of growth, potion of healing, potion of greater healing, potion of superior healing, potion of supreme healing, potion of heroism, potion of invisibility, potion of mind reading, potion of poison, potion of resistance, potion of speed, potion of water breathing, restorative ointment, sovereign glue, universal solvent.

P-8. Alchemical Bazaar

While several permanent alchemical businesses are located throughout Cat's Cradle, this large open plaza offers the opportunity for individual alchemists, smaller enterprises, and other less influential sellers to provide their wares to the general public, and conversely provides shoppers with the chance to find bargains and obtain unusual alchemical products that may not be available elsewhere. The bazaar consists mostly of a broad paved plaza with booths and small wooden structures around the outer edge, and is located conveniently close to the Panhandle Docks so that cargo can be brought here directly from incoming vessels.

Each day, the bazaar fills with sellers who either occupy rented booths and structures or spread their wares out on the pavement for sale. In the latter case, selling space is first come, first served, and canny sellers show up before dawn with their goods, groundcloths, assistants and money chests, ready to grab prime real estate at the bazaar.

At sunup, a city watch member strikes a large bell located near the bazaar's entrance, triggering an influx of eager customers. During the bright days of spring and summer, the bazaar is a noisy, colorful riot as sellers loudly proclaim the quality of their wares, buyers shout questions and negotiators bargain, expressing mock anger at prices set too high or offers that are seen as too low. Money and goods change hands, buyers of all social levels thread their way through the crowds while loaded with purchases, sellers argue with customers and with each other, and of course pickpockets run wild, using the press of the crowd to avoid overworked watch members, most of whom consider the bazaar to be little more than punishment duty.

The bazaar closes at midnight, or at least when the weary city watch decides to ring the bell again to signal that it is time for the plaza's remaining occupants to complete transactions, pack up, and go home. Early in the morning, once the plaza is empty, it is swept and cleaned by a crew hired by the watch from among Cat's Cradle's poorer citizens, work which needs to be completed by the ringing of the first bell of the following dawn.

P-9. Panhandle Docks

These durable stone docks were built by dwarven engineers almost a century ago in the wake of the Dockside Fire, in which an alchemical accident destroyed much of Cat's Cradle's waterfront. While mundane cargo and nonvolatile alchemy components are ordinarily shipped through the main docks, the Panhandle Docks are reserved for dangerous, unstable, rare, or valuable cargoes, carefully offloaded by professional dockworkers licensed and certified by the barony, both by hand labor and with sturdy cranes.

Incoming cargoes are carefully inspected and matched against cargo manifests, fees are levied, and official seals affixed before they can be transported to their purchasers or taken to the warehouse for storage. The entire neighborhood has become vital to Cat's Cradle's continued economic survival and so has come under the separate administration of its own noble manager, **Count Arzend** (see **Location P-13**), who is answerable only to his ally and friend the baron.

P-10. Panhandle Gate

This portal is generally kept open at all hours and is well guarded, as it is the only city gate through which volatile or dangerous alchemical substances can be shipped. Inspectors are stationed here, ready to check out any cargoes, levy fees, and provide certification that the incoming items are safely packed and bound for the proper recipient.

P-11. Customs House

An extensive bureaucracy has grown up around the need to manage, document and apply appropriate taxes and fees to the substances that come in and out of the city. Under Customs Minister **Charlerat Hussan**, the organization has grown to more than 50 employees, the largest it has ever been. Hussan is a humorless bureaucrat with no apparent family or interests outside his job. He's intensely disliked by the other customs employees, but as the baron has frequently noted, he gets results and income from tariffs, fees, and taxes on cargoes has been flowing into the barony's coffers in greater quantities under his administration.

Customs inspectors are expected to be honest, dependable, and loyal, and have access to all cargoes at the Panhandle and the main Lake Docks. They are expected to oversee all cargoes, check manifests and levy fees, and collect them on the spot and transport them back to the Customs House, where they are kept in the cellar vault before being taken to Cat's Cradle.

P-12. Waterfront Warehouse

A group of alchemists own this structure and use it to store inert, safe, or mundane cargo from the nearby docks. While the main Alchemical Shipping Warehouse is the more expensive alternative for valuable or dangerous items, this facility provides cheaper and less heavily secured storage, and space is available for rent by other customers.

Adventure Hook: A cargo brought to the warehouse was contaminated with monstrous eggs of some kind, and the brood has hatched. This could range from giant spiders for lower-level adventurers to something far worse for higher-level adventurers.

P-13. Count Arzend's Residence

The Panhandle is the only Cat's Cradle district to boast its own governor, and **Count Arzend**, a personal friend and powerful ally of Baron Scale, takes the job with all seriousness. Arzend, his wife Cassia, and their two children have made their home in his assigned district. Their home is a converted government ministry building that allows for comfortable daily life as well as providing extensive space for business and governmental administration. The residence sees a continual stream of traffic in and out as officials, guild members, alchemists, merchants, nobles, and others visit to meet with each other and with the count himself.

While the combined quarters are efficient, the situation has begun to take a toll on Arzend's family. The house is highly secure with constant shifts of guards and an extensive password-based pass system. Arzend and his family are extremely valuable individuals and are never allowed to leave the residence without escort. Countess Cassia has grown bored and weary of her surroundings and the tedium of life as a virtual prisoner, while their twin children Magdra and Jacq, age eight, feel similarly cooped up and frustrated, wishing to have friends their own age and a more normal life than that of a powerful nobleman.

Adventure Hook: Count Arzend is willing to use private agents when he feels that his ordinary resources might not be independent or resourceful enough to handle the task he has in mind. In general, any type of hook involving ships or cargo would be appropriate to use here.

SURROUNDING REGION

The region surrounding Cat's Cradle is unique, though it does not look at all special on most maps. Particularities of the area are outlined below, but the strangest feature of the surrounding land is its total lack of all disease, including plagues, blights, and any illness that affects living plants or animals. Pest infestations can still occur, but these do not carry disease. Even magical diseases are prevented unless they are caused by a curse. Visitors to the area do not benefit from this blessing, but long-term residents all eventually do.

Some believe that Cat's Cradle and its surrounding wilderness will one day pay a terrible price for this immunity, but most would prefer to accept the gift and live their lives in illness-free ignorance of its source.

S-1. THE BARONIAL FARMS

The barons of Cat's Cradle are deeded a wide swath of land, larger than some counties, though sparsely populated. Nearly all land near Cat's Cradle that isn't forest, mine, or quarry, therefore, is designated as baronial farmland.

As is always the case with hereditary leadership, the tenant farmers on baronial land have had many different lots in life over the centuries, depending on the whims of the current baron or baron's liege, the wisdom of current land management, and the vagaries of seasonal weather conditions. Current baronial tenants are enjoying quite a surge in prosperity due to a series of abundant years in a row, intelligent agricultural planning on the part of current leadership, and extremely fair and reasonable taxation on the part of Baron Scale.

The current baron is very popular in the countryside, perhaps even more so than in the city proper, though those northern farms closest to the Forest of Cantricle are beginning to grow nervous about the rumors of banditry therein. Petitions to the baron for stronger protection near the forest are beginning to pour in since last winter.

S-2. THE CARAVAN ROUTES

Most of Cat's Cradle's commerce travels along the Great Hyon River. However, there are also regular caravans to surrounding towns, including the rival town of Five-and-Copper to the east, and a town called Sundry to the west. A second caravan route runs north through the Forest of Cantricle to the town of Voles, and south to the town of Dancers.

In order to avoid disrupting river traffic, no bridges have been built across the Great Hyon in the Cat's Cradle region, and the north-south caravan instead uses a ferry east of the city (past the lake) to cross the river. A massive bridge, tall enough to allow the largest rivercraft, is planned to be constructed in the nearby village of Gambit in future, as Gambit's geography lends itself better to such an undertaking, but for now, the eastern ferry functions well enough, save in the worst weather.

S-3. THE COTTAGE

The Cottage is an old baronial hunting lodge that hasn't been used by the family in generations. By tradition, the baron occasionally sends out a work crew to at least make certain that the place is not a security hazard to forest travelers, but in recent years such crews have faced repeated misfortunes, accidents, and other difficulties, such that the Cottage is now reputed to be cursed.

Of course, a more rational explanation might be that the forest bandits are using the Cottage as a hideout and taking pains to make certain that the baron's servants don't find them there, but if so, no direct evidence of this has yet been made public, so the rumors of a curse are left to grow more outlandish with each passing tale.

S-4. DEEP LAKE

A very deep portion of the Hyon River just outside the docks of Cat's Cradle is part of the reason the harbor remains calm even during foul weather. Residents of Cat's Cradle have been calling this area "Deep Lake" for centuries.

Deep Lake is known for several things. First, it is unnaturally deep for a lake that is barely more than a wide patch of a river. Second, the deepest parts of Deep Lake are perilous in the extreme. Much mystery and superstition surrounds Deep Lake, as the nature of its peril is not well understood, but all merchants and river captains who travel the region know that you never sail or row small vessels through the center of the lake, nor even along its southern shore if possible.

As for what happens to vessels that break the rules and enter the deeper lake, no coherent witness accounts have been recorded. Observers from the safer parts of the lake have seen only a great splashing, followed by the destruction of the vessel in question. There have never been survivors, even from military expeditions. Remains of the crafts themselves usually wash up on the southern lake shore eventually, but remains of people or livestock (or fish) aboard are never found, leading most to believe that these are being eaten by a monster.

The late Dessa Showe, an expert on the Salchamp who reportedly went mad before her disappearance on Deep Lake, was known to believe that the lake was formed in the same ancient conflict that created the Salt Skeleton. She wrote that some titanic blow must have sundered the ground beside the Great Hyon, resulting in the lake's strange topography. Showe never wrote about her beliefs surrounding the "lake monster," but considering her otherwise inexplicable choice to row out over the lake all alone, many believe that her final year of research — of which no documentation remains — was all about the lake monster and its connection to the Salt Skeleton and other quirks of the Cat's Cradle region.

S-5. FOREST OF CANTRICLE

To the north of Cat's Cradle stands the southern edge of the Forest of Cantricle. The caravan route between Cat's Cradle and the town of Voles, to the north, lies through this forest. It is, for the most part, an ordinary and friendly forest, cleared long ago of large, magical predators or other supernatural dangers by the army of a previous queen.

However, since the end of the Salt War, the remains of the bandit army that attempted to wrest control of the Salchamp from Cat's Cradle are known to have hidden in the forest to lick their wounds. The late Baron Escallel gave his life in the final battle that slew the bandit lord and broke the back of the invaders. It was a crushing victory for Cat's Cradle, but in the end, not all the key bandit leaders were slain or taken captive. It is believed that their numbers are growing once more within the forest (perhaps in response to unrest in other parts of the kingdom), and caravans heading north are hiring more security than they have in decades in response to rumors of disappearances and assaults in the forest.

Adventure Hook: It is said that Baron Scale is consulting with surrounding lords to form a long-term strategy for ousting the bandits from the forest. The characters might be recruited into this effort at any level of expertise.

S-6. THE JADE-MARBLE QUARRY

First discovered some 150 years ago by Salchamp miners, the jade-marble quarry takes up parts of what has come to be known as Cat's Hill, wherever the Salchamp is played out. Behind and beneath the alchemical salts, there seems to always be a long, mostly straight vein of this jade green marble-like stone. As such, the jade-marble quarry looks more like a mine than a typical quarry, but the name has stuck.

Jade-marble has been run through a long battery of alchemical tests and has shown signs over the course of its use in Cat's Cradle of being even more durable than ordinary marble, or than similar-looking green stone from other parts of the world. It seems clear that the difficulties associated with ripplestone will never recur with jade-marble. That said, the jade-marble supply near Cat's Cradle seems already to be running thin, and is currently valued more highly than its weight in gold. Jade-marble quarriers are looking for work in other related trades, but many hope that a new jade-marble vein will be discovered when the current Salchamp begins to play out, as has happened in the past.

According to Dessa Showe's maps, however, it seems likely that jade-marble is a quite limited resource and that, however plentiful it may have seemed while the Jade District was being built, there may not be much of it left to find — not near Cat's Cradle at any rate.

S-7. THE MILLETON ESTATE

Though primarily known in recent generations for their glassworks in Bricktown district, the Milleton family have also been land tenants of the Cat's Cradle barons for many generations. Their farm is a prosperous one, and the Milletons were wealthy even before founding their glassworks — so wealthy as to dwarf the fortunes of many minor aristocrats in the region.

Wealth and success notwithstanding, however, the Milleton family has entered an unfortunate period in its history. Large and sprawling, with literally hundreds of members, the Milletons work their lands and glassworks themselves, only rarely hiring help from outside. This increases their profits, as no wages need to be paid to workers, but it has also created a cold and businesslike culture within

*NOT ON MAP
THE TOWN OF
Cat's Cradle
MAP S

the family, including a strict hierarchy of privilege and authority, depending upon one's relationship to the matriarch, Landra Milleton.

Landra is shrewd and sharp-witted, even at 95 years of age (human), and has built up the Milleton fortunes dramatically. She maintains close ties with many Jade District bigwigs and other wealthy allies, and seems to see every plot against her coming from leagues away. She is also, however, known to force her relatives into whatever roles the family needs, regardless of their own inclinations, to maintain tight control over the family purse. She doles out rewards only where it suits her plans to do so and keeps her relatives dependent upon her for their very livelihoods.

Milletons who take family matters to the watch or the baron are, of course, cut off without a copper. The Milleton intrigues stay within the family and, as such, it has been difficult for Cat's Cradle authorities to intervene.

Adventure Hook: The Milletons wait with bated breath for their fierce matriarch to finally die and leave the family leadership to a new generation (though, of course, Landra's eldest children are in their 70s, so "new" is a relative term). It seems to suit Grandmother Landra's purposes (or perhaps her underlying sadistic nature) to watch her relatives squabble amongst themselves, and so the Milleton estate has spiraled ever further into a nightmare realm of power-jockeying, plot and counter-plot, blackmail, framing, kidnappings, and even murders.

S-8. The Old Quarry

Out near the Salchamp stands the hollow and near-abandoned ditches of the old ripplestone quarry. Due to the associated shame of the great ripplestone debacle, few are willing to go near the place, though in truth, ripplestone remains a serviceable, decorative stone for small indoor art pieces, figurines, and the like.

Officially speaking, the poorly maintained and slowly dissolving ripplestone quarry is too dangerous to work, and by baronial order is to be left to return to nature. In reality, however, it is not uncommon to see or hear workers with their picks and hammers, late at night, still harvesting stones from the more sheltered sections of the quarry. The baronial constabulary occasionally "puts a stop" to such activities, but they always seem to crop up again within a few months, and rumor has it that the Thieves' Guild — and particularly the goons working for Ox's Labor — don't take kindly to those who rat out ripplestone quarry operations.

S-9. Orfell's Smithy

To the immediate east of Cat's Cradle stands a small, walled facility known as Orfell's Smithy. Begun generations ago by a local folk hero named Orfell the Smith, this is the largest and best known ironworks in the Cat's Cradle region. Leadership of the smithy and training of its apprentices are appointed by the baron, rather than inherited within a family, and the current smithy administration is considered shrewd and skilled.

Orfell's Smithy is only famous on a local level, with its steel being considered of good but hardly legendary quality elsewhere. Cat's Cradle is known for stone and alchemical salts, not iron, so it has been many generations since the smithy has turned a truly impressive profit for the baron. Nevertheless, it does well enough, and due to its weapons production capabilities is considered an important military asset for Cat's Cradle's defense. As such, the smithy walls are high, thick, and in good repair, and the smithy is always well-stocked and well-defended.

Some believe that an old escape tunnel leads from Cat's Keep to Orfell's Smithy, but no known maps depict such a route if it exists.

S-10. The Salchamp

Discovered not long after the first ripplestone vein, the Salchamp has since become Cat's Cradle's most important source of income. Its presence in the region is also the reason Cat's Cradle has become so important a hub for alchemical research.

The salts mined from the Salchamp are not truly salts in any mineral sense of the term. Rather, they are alchemical salts with varying complex properties that can be brought to full potential by alchemical processes and combinations. The salts come in all colors, but green is the most common.

Some decades ago, after mapping the known salt veins through the hillsides surrounding Cat's Cradle, an alchemist by the name of Dessa Showe put forth the theory that an ancient titan or god, while wounded, somehow fused with the earth in this place and left behind a large chunk of its own flesh upon departure. Fused with the earth as it was, this flesh did not decompose normally, but was transformed into stone and "salts" and eventually was covered over by ordinary soil, only to be rediscovered and mined by Cat's Cradle centuries later.

According to this theory, both ripplestone and Cat's Cradle's jade-marble quarries are related to this same phenomenon, though both lack the mystical properties of the alchemical salts. According to Showe, the ripplestone might be part of the departed titan's raiment or perhaps fur, the jade-marble its bones, and the salts its flesh, blood, and organs.

Ordinary miners tend to reject this theory as absurd, and often bristle when they hear the Salchamp's other common name: the Salt Skeleton. Instead, the word among salt-miners is that these are just special rocks and minerals to be mined like any other. But it is undeniable that the maps of the various "veins" and deposits do seem unusually organic in their shape, not unlike a giant chunk of petrified flesh and bone.

Showe also believed that the presence of the Salchamp so near Cat's Cradle was the reason that disease had become so rare in the town. She cautioned, however, that this immunity would one day come with a dire consequence upon which she never elaborated. At the age of 56, after a year of particularly immersive research, Dessa Showe is said to have abruptly lost her mind, rowed herself out to the middle of Deep Lake (**Location S-4**), and disappeared. She left no notes of her final year of research.

S-11. The Witch's Hut

A humble stone hut entirely covered in verdant greenery stands near the southern edge of the Forest of Cantricle. This place is known as the Witch's Hut and is given a wide berth by local travelers. In reality, this hut is occupied by an old elven druid, with land rights officially granted by the baron, but she does tend to be an antisocial sort and has a tendency to deliberately scare away visitors whenever possible or to make herself impossible to find. She pays her taxes to the lord of the land, however, and — if approached with cautious courtesy — is willing to come to Cat's Cradle's defense as needed, so long as Cat's Cradle's leadership continues to treat the forest and surrounding wilderness with respect.

She has been framed for crimes against representatives of the baron in the past, but no wrongdoing on her part has ever been proven. Those in the know understand her to have been instrumental in Cat's Cradle's victory against the bandits in the Salt War. Nevertheless, the rumor persists that she is a dangerous witch, and Baron Scale seems unable to convince her that she should not continue to play into such tales with her antisocial behavior.

S-12. Miners' Shanties

The southern edge of the Cantricle Forest is home to a small town of miners' shanties. Most of these are temporary structures, and the area resembles a camp more than a permanent settlement. The shanties are not policed by town authorities, which makes for a very lawless area.

Adventure Hook: One or more miners have had their shanties robbed by bandits in the Cantricle. They need someone to track down the thieves — probably local bandits — and recover their stolen hoards of alchemical salt.

9 781943 067855